"This wasn't an accident!" Annie burst out

"Someone harmed the painting deliberately!"

Derrek's face went cold and hard. "That's not your concern."

"But I just don't understand how anybody could do this to a painting, could hurt it like this...."

"Paintings can't feel," Derrek said, his voice rough. "People are what's important—or don't you believe that, Annie?"

She recoiled from the scorn in his voice. "Of course I believe that," she said angrily. "I'm just trying to figure out what happened."

"You want to know the story, don't you, Annie? You want a logical explanation, something neat and tidy to file away."

She shook her head helplessly. "No, I—"

"It's not a story for you, Annie Brooke." His mouth twisted in a humorless smile. "Just restore the painting and don't ask any more questions."

Ellen James has wanted a writing career ever since she won a national short-story competition in high school. *The Turquoise Heart*, set in Ellen's home state of New Mexico, is her second Romance. She and her husband, both writers, love to travel, and they share an interest in wildlife photography and in American history.

Books by Ellen James

HARLEQUIN ROMANCE
3052—HOME FOR LOVE

Don't miss any of our special offers. Write to us at the following address for information on our newest releases.

Harlequin Reader Service
901 Fuhrmann Blvd., P.O. Box 1397, Buffalo, NY 14240
Canadian address: P.O. Box 603,
Fort Erie, Ont. L2A 5X3

THE TURQUOISE HEART

Ellen James

Harlequin Books

TORONTO • NEW YORK • LONDON
AMSTERDAM • PARIS • SYDNEY • HAMBURG
STOCKHOLM • ATHENS • TOKYO • MILAN

ISBN 0-373-03069-X

Harlequin Romance first edition August 1990

CHAPTER ONE

ANNIE BROOKE stretched herself out rigidly in the lounge chair, sunglasses in place. The hot dry New Mexico sun shone overhead and glinted off the water of the hotel swimming pool. Two teenage girls in bikinis floated by. Annie pulled up the strap of her own modest tank suit and pressed her head back against the chair's plastic pillow. She'd given herself the project of relaxing for an hour, and with determination she unclenched the muscles of her jaw. Like everything else, there was a method to relaxation. A person just had to be systematic about it.

Annie closed her eyes and concentrated on her toes, willing them to go limp one by one. R-e-l-a-x, she told her feet. Relax! They started to obey her, but then her jaw tensed up again. Annie wiggled her toes in frustration. As if she'd summoned a genie, two warm hands wrapped themselves around her feet and gently began massaging them.

She yanked off her sunglasses and struggled to a sitting position. She stared at the man who was holding her feet, her gaze caught by the vivid blue of his eyes. His hair was a deep black, curling at his nape and forehead. Bold irregular features dominated his face, the type of features a sculptor would immediately want to capture in stone or clay. He was kneeling beside her

...ew he would be very tall when
...n smiled lazily at Annie, and all
...p staring back at him. His fin-
...her feet a tantalizing massage.
..." he murmured, his voice deep
...oosen up your muscles, Annabel
Brooke."

Annie detested her given name, and hearing it spo-
ken stirred her from this odd bemusement. She tried
tugging her feet away from him, but he only held them
more tightly. She tossed back her brown shoulder-
length hair and frowned at him.

"Oh...you must be with the Richards Foundation," she said to the man. "But you're much too
early to drive me to Santa Fe. I was told you wouldn't
be here until later this morning."

He shrugged imperturbably. "Plans change, Annabel." He smiled again and traced a finger lightly
over her arch. A shiver, half delicious, half fearful, ran
through Annie and she jerked her feet away decisively. She stood up but the man stayed kneeling, his
weight on the heels of his cowboy boots.

"You know, I've seen you before, Annabel," he
remarked, "hiding out in the kitchen at the museum
banquet last month. You don't like socializing much,
do you?" He leaned his head back to give her a leisurely perusal. She felt self-conscious in her bathing
suit and abruptly sat down again.

"I hate all those banquets and social functions," she
declared. "The Darcy Museum doesn't need a lot of
people running around in tuxedos and cluttering up
the place."

"Those are my feelings exactly," he said. "There's nothing worse than a tuxedo." His tone was serious, but amusement sparked underneath it. Annie glared at him. Everything had gone wrong with this trip from the very beginning. Her plane had been so late flying into Albuquerque last night that she hadn't got to bed until midnight. And somehow she'd forgotten to bring along the mystery novel she was reading, right when she'd reached the point where the villain would be revealed. To top it all off, this man was harassing her!

She didn't want to be in New Mexico at all, that was the worst of it. She wanted to be back in Denver at the Caroline Darcy Museum where she belonged. The director of the museum was retiring, and Annie had put in her application for the vacant post. If she were chosen for the job, she would be able to fulfill her dreams for the museum.

Annie was currently art conservator there, and her specialty was restoring damaged paintings. She often traveled to different locations so that an injured work of art would not have to risk transportation. That was the reason she'd come to New Mexico. Her presence had been commanded by one of the museum trustees, Mr. D. F. Richards, so that she could restore a painting for his art foundation. Ordinarily Annie enjoyed the assignments that took her to new places, but with the job of director opening up, this was the worst possible time for her to leave Denver.

"Chocolate, that's the right word," the man said, nodding to himself as if in satisfaction.

"What?" Annie eyed him uncertainly.

"Rich dark chocolate. That's the color of your hair, and your eyes, too. But I forgot to introduce myself.

I'm Derrek Richards, Annabel.'' He held out his hand and she automatically gave it a firm shake.

"Derrek—you mean you're D. F. Richards, the museum trustee...." Now she was really chagrined. She had wanted to present herself with a certain amount of dignity when she met him, but here she was, all slathered in sunscreen. She glowered at him, feeling that she had to explain herself. "Mr. Richards, I really didn't expect anyone to pick me up until a few hours from now. Of course, I would've gone straight to Santa Fe to meet you if there had been a direct flight from Denver. I do believe in efficiency, and I don't like to waste time. That's why I'm out here by the pool—I'm doing a relaxation project."

"That's what relaxation is to you—a project you're supposed to complete?" he asked.

"Too many people don't make time for it," she asserted. "At any rate, that's why I'm out here. But now that you've arrived, I'll just go change—"

"There's no hurry. Tell me about yourself, Annabel Brooke."

"I go by Annie," she said briskly. "I've worked at the museum for nine years now, and last year I completed my degree in art history at the University of Colorado." She could not keep a hint of pride out of her voice; it had taken so much to struggle through school, commuting to Boulder for classes while she held down her full-time job.

"Nine years at the museum," he echoed in a tone of disbelief. "You must have been a kid when you started."

"I was seventeen. I swept the floors in the gift shop, and I went for doughnuts whenever anybody wanted some." She smiled, remembering.

"That's quite a jump, from gofer to art conservator," Derrek observed.

Annie nodded confidently. "I knew exactly what I wanted at the museum, and I went after it," she said. "I worked my way through a long apprenticeship with Jim Lawrence, the conservator back then. He taught me everything I know about art restoration." She spoke with affection and respect; Jim was retired now.

Derrek regarded Annie speculatively. "The museum means a great deal to you, doesn't it?" he asked. "Worth any sacrifice."

"As a matter of fact, yes, that's exactly how I feel." Annie spoke fervently, and there was an awkward pause after her words. She saw the way Derrek's eyes went hard, a shuttered expression coming over his face as if he'd lost any interest in speaking to her. Annie clenched her fists in frustration. She wasn't any good with people, that was the problem. She didn't know how to talk to them; her dedication to her work always came through too stridently. All her co-workers at the museum thought she was cold and unfeeling, thought she didn't care about people—that she was perfectly happy in a world of paintings alone.

It hurt when others said those things about her. She knew she was reserved; her lonely childhood had eventually taught her to welcome solitude rather than to fear it. She worked best on her own, without supervision or even companionship. But that didn't mean she was cold and unfeeling. She had many feelings bottled up inside—she just didn't know how to express them!

Now Derrek unfolded himself from the ground and stood up. His frame was lean but muscular, clothed in faded jeans and a blue plaid shirt of worn cotton. The blue accentuated his vivid eyes. He took Annie's hand and pulled her up to stand next to him. She stared at his chest, a warmth spreading through her from the touch of his fingers. But his voice was expressionless as he spoke to her.

"Well, Annie Brooke, let's get on with what you came here to do." He seemed to be challenging her in some way, treating her with a peculiar intimacy although they'd barely met. Annie tugged her hand free.

"I'll be ready to leave for Santa Fe in a few minutes," she said. "I'll meet you in the lobby."

"Fine," he answered, his tone brusque. Annie turned and strode away from him. But it was impossible to look dignified in a swimsuit, her bare feet padding across tiles. She was positive she felt Derrek's gaze move up and down the entire length of her anatomy. At the door to the hotel she turned and looked back at him defiantly. But he wasn't watching her at all. Even the two girls splashing hopefully in the pool didn't attract his attention. He stood with his hands in the pockets of his jeans, head bent in abstraction. Annie wondered what thoughts could be so engrossing.

She went up to her room and dressed quickly in the jacket and skirt she'd worn on the plane. Then she stood in front of the mirror to brush out her hair. It was thick and glossy, but Annie had always thought of it as an ordinary brown. Not rich dark chocolate.

She combed her bangs down over her forehead. Straightening the collar of her navy jacket, she gave herself one last inspection. Her brown eyes gazed solemnly back at her from the mirror; her face was pale in spite of her foray into the southwestern sun. But her nose was strong and straight, and her chin was molded in decisive lines. Only her mouth betrayed her businesslike image. It was too full and lush, a natural shade of deep rose, and Annie always tried to tone it down with subdued lipstick. She was being especially careful about that today. Everything else was in order—her hair curled under obediently and her white blouse was fresh after spending the night on a hanger. She looked neat and well-groomed, just as she always did.

Annie turned away from her reflection and checked that everything was packed in her suitcase. She grabbed hold of it with one hand, balancing her two large boxes of equipment in her arms. It was an awkward load but it was also a precious one, and Annie preferred to carry it herself. Inside these boxes were the many tools she used to restore damaged paintings. She took slow measured steps as she made her way down to the lobby, peering around the boxes to see where she was going.

Derrek came forward quickly to unburden her. She held on to her boxes.

"Don't worry—I have them," she said, but he grasped them from the other side. For a moment he and Annie were involved in a restrained tug of war.

"Don't be ridiculous," he muttered. Annie held on as long as she could, giving up only when her equipment began to rattle. Arms free, she headed for the hotel desk.

"I've paid your bill," Derrek said. "All your expenses will be covered by the Richards Foundation while you're in New Mexico."

Annie gave a slight grimace. That was the customary business arrangement when she traveled, but somehow this time it made her feel obligated.

She saw Derrek glancing quizzically at the boxes he was balancing. They weren't made of plain ordinary cardboard; one was patterned in green and yellow stripes, the other was a bright red. Derrek looked as if he was bearing large enticing Christmas presents.

"Those boxes are just right for my equipment," Annie explained hastily. "They have partitions inside, and their own handles. They're really quite practical."

"Does everything have to be practical with you?" Derrek asked wryly. "Even red boxes?"

"Of course," she answered. "Everything has its purpose—that's just the way life is."

He shook his head, but led the way out to the parking lot. He loaded Annie's boxes and suitcase into the back of an open four-wheel-drive Jeep. Annie tried maneuvering herself into the passenger seat, but was hindered by her narrow skirt. Derrek watched with interest as she attempted to hop into the seat rear end first. When her efforts failed, she did her best to ignore his amused gaze. Now she faced the Jeep and considered the possibility of catapulting herself upward. Darn this skirt! And why couldn't D. F. Richards have a nice low car?

"Need some help?" Derrek asked obligingly.

"Yes." She turned toward him. "You could drive over to that loading dock around the side of the building. I'll be able to climb in from there without any trouble." She was pleased with this solution, but Derrek only laughed. Before she knew what he was about, he put both hands around her waist and lifted her easily into the Jeep. He held on to her a moment longer than necessary, his face close to hers.

"If you want to be practical, Annie Brooke, you'd better get yourself some blue jeans. This is rough country out here." He spoke lazily, mockingly, but again Annie sensed the challenge in his voice.

"I can handle anything that comes my way," she declared.

"We'll see," he murmured, his eyes lingering on her face. Then he went around to the driver's side, whistling a low tune. Annie buckled her seat belt, glad when they were on the highway and driving out of Albuquerque. She wanted to reach Santa Fe and get down to business as soon as possible. She had come here to restore a painting, not to spar with a disturbing man like Derrek Richards.

The wind whipped her hair as the Jeep bounced along. Annie gave up trying to hold it in place with her hand and reached into her purse for an elastic band. Soon she had an absurd ponytail that stuck out behind her, but at least she was free to look around. The broad highway curved its way between mountains. There was no snow here, as in the mountains outside Denver; spring had already arrived full force in New Mexico.

"This is Tijeras Canyon," Derrek told her. "Scissors Canyon. Looks pretty peaceful now, but a couple of centuries ago you might have seen Comanche raiders galloping through here."

Annie glanced at him. "You sound envious," she commented. "Do you wish you could have been one of those raiders?"

He chuckled. "I like hearing stories about them, but I wouldn't have fit in. I'm too easygoing."

Annie had already sensed this—Derrek Richards seemed to be a man who preferred to move at his own casual pace through life. She sat back and reflected on what little she'd heard about him. His father, Carlisle Richards, had been a talented and famous painter. As head of his own foundation, Carlisle had donated generously to the museum and had served as one of its trustees. Upon his death some months ago, Derrek had stepped in to take over at the foundation, as well as to assume the position of trustee.

"Are you an artist like your father was?" Annie asked now. It seemed a natural question, but immediately Derrek's expression went dark.

"No, I'm not," he said curtly, his tone forbidding further discussion. Tension hardened the lines of his profile. Annie felt confused; Derrek Richards was a complex man, not easily fathomed. She didn't speak for a while, and it was Derrek who broke the silence as they turned onto another highway.

"From here on we'll be following the Turquoise Trail," he said. "There's a quicker way to reach Santa Fe, but this is the route I always choose. It's got quite an interesting history. Turquoise was mined out here for hundreds of years and that's how the road got its nickname. But the Turquoise Trail means something much more than that to me. Adventure, magic, whatever you want to call it. Look around and maybe you'll see what I mean."

Although she didn't believe in magic, Annie was caught up by his words. She did look around carefully. The road narrowed, passed through a small village and then left human habitation behind. Dark green scrub trees spread out on both sides, and dusky mountains rose in the distance.

"This is all piñon and juniper," Derrek said. "But you'll see a lot of other things if you know what to look for—that's cholla cactus over there, with the yellow blooms. And the plants that look like big feather dusters—those are rabbitbrush, or chamisa." He made the names sound like poetry. It was a beautiful landscape, lonely and wild, and punctuated with color. After a while Derrek pulled over to the side of the road, close to a stream that wound its way through a shallow gully. When he cut the engine Annie could hear the rustle of the breeze and the raucous call of birds. No other cars came along the road; this place belonged to nature alone.

"What are we doing here?" Annie asked, the sound of her own voice jarring her. "Why did you stop?"

"No special reason," Derrek said. "Maybe I just wanted to enjoy the scenery." He swung out of his side of the Jeep. Annie slid down from her own seat before he could put his hands around her waist again. She followed him, stepping cautiously over the ground in her navy pumps. They came to a barbed-wire fence.

"You first," Derrek said gallantly, lifting up one of the wires. She looked at the sharp ends poking out of it.

"Is this really necessary?" she asked.

"No, it's not," he conceded, "but you might actually have fun if you give yourself a chance."

With a beleaguered sigh Annie worked her way through the fence. She felt one of the barbs catch on her jacket, but it was too late; the material ripped as she stumbled through to the other side.

Derrek straddled the fence with ease and loped down to the stream. Annie struggled out of her jacket, plunking herself down on a broad flat rock. She had a run in her hose and her hair was sliding loose from its ponytail. She was a mess, something she wasn't used to being at all. But Derrek didn't seem to notice her disarray. He took a stone and sent it skipping into the stream. The feathery chamisa waved gently in the breeze; the sky was a clear thin blue, like watercolor. It was so peaceful here, and Annie's muscles gradually relaxed. If she *had* believed in magic, she would have sworn that Derrek Richards was casting some sort of spell over her. She stretched out her legs, her eyes half closing. Sunlight shimmered on the stream, lulling her still further.

"I was right," Derrek said softly.

"About what?" Annie murmured.

"You're enjoying yourself in a completely impractical way."

She opened her eyes quickly and straightened her back.

"I'm not enjoying myself that much," she retorted. "You should be grateful I'm the kind of person who likes to get down to business. Why don't you tell me about the painting you want restored? I should have had more information about it before I left Denver."

"We'll get to that soon enough." His voice was taut, and he skipped another stone onto the stream. "Are you like this at the museum, Annie? Always ready to get down to business?"

"I'm a hard worker," she said. "I've had to be. And now it's going to be more important than ever for me to work hard. I'm sure you know that the director of the museum is retiring and I've applied for the position."

"Yes, I know all about that." His eyes traveled over her. "Do you really think you're the best applicant for the job?"

"In many ways, yes," she affirmed. "No one else knows the museum as well as I do, or cares as much about it."

"What about Vance Forester?" Derrek asked. "He's already assistant director, and he's also applied. He seems the most likely candidate."

Annie's fingers tightened on her jacket. She detested breezy charming Vance Forester. She had made the mistake of going out with him several times, and all he had wanted was a breezy physical relationship. Neither Annie's heart nor her body had responded to Vance, and she'd rejected him point-blank. But it seemed that Vance wasn't used to rejection. He had retaliated, telling Annie she was frigid. That had hit her hard, for deep down she feared it was true. No man had ever touched her heart or aroused her passion. Was something wrong with her?

She struggled to give Derrek an objective response about Vance. "He is in line to be director," she said. "I'm not denying that. But he's only worked at the museum for a short time. He doesn't know it the way I do." She lifted her hands. "You see, it's not just the fact that I started there when I was seventeen. I found the museum even before that." She hesitated.

"Tell me about it," Derrek urged.

After a moment Annie spoke again, musingly, almost to herself. "I remember that first day so perfectly," she said. "I'd just turned fourteen and I was wandering around so I wouldn't have to go home right after school. Then I looked up and I saw this big wonderful old Victorian mansion, all redbrick and tucked away behind a wrought-iron fence. Caroline Darcy Museum—Visitors Welcome, the sign said. It was like a personal invitation, waiting there just for me.'' Annie shrugged, uncomfortable at revealing so much about herself.

"Go on,'' Derrek prodded gently.

She smiled. "I went up the steps and I found a whole new world. All those beautiful paintings, each one offering me something of its own, just waiting to be explored. Right then I knew I'd found my place in life, and after that I went to the museum almost every weekend. It was like a home for me, in a way. I'd sit and look at all those paintings for hours, and each one was different and special. Sometimes that's what kept me going as a teenager, knowing that I had my own retreat, my own escape.'' She stopped abruptly. Why had she allowed all these feelings to spill out?

Derrek was watching her intently. "What did you want to escape from, Annie?'' he asked. She gazed at the muddy toes of her pumps, determined not to expose any more of her memories. Growing up, she had learned to be reserved, to keep her emotions hidden. She didn't know how to be any other way.

"It was all a long time ago,'' she said lightly. "None of it really matters now. We were talking about Vance. I think he's competent, but I have something special to offer. I have so many ideas about where the museum should be headed. Right now it's stagnating.'' Annie shook her head ruefully. "I've been trying so hard to change things, but I haven't had the power. Last year when the job of assistant director came up, I applied for that, too. But the trustees went outside the museum and chose Vance. He's a man, for one thing. Seems that was in his favor.''

Derrek leaned against a fence post and regarded her incredulously. "That probably didn't have anything to do with it," he said.

Annie stared up at him, shading her eyes with her hand. "I've been competing against men my entire career," she said. "I know what I'm talking about. Men tend to stick together and close ranks. No one in a position of power at the museum is a woman. The last one who had any influence was Caroline Darcy, and she founded the place."

Derrek shrugged. "The trustees are all fair-minded, as far as I can tell. They just want to pick the best people to administer the museum."

Annie struggled to her feet. "All I've ever wanted was a chance to prove myself," she said hotly. "I could do that if I were director. I could do a lot of things!"

Derrek watched her thoughtfully. "All you have to do is convince the trustees of your talents," he said after a moment. "But that's something you already know, isn't it?"

His close scrutiny made Annie feel off balance. Again she sensed he was challenging her somehow, putting her on the defensive. She came back with her own challenge.

"Why do you keep saying 'the trustees' like you're not one yourself?" she demanded. "You're probably as close-minded as the rest of them!"

"Hold on a minute—I'm an architect by trade. I only took on the foundation and the job as trustee because I was railroaded into it." His voice was grim, and Annie looked at him in surprise. He was such a forceful man. She couldn't imagine anyone coercing him into doing something he didn't want to do.

"You don't really care about the museum, then," she said disapprovingly.

"No, that's not it. I like your Caroline Darcy Museum well enough. I've always admired old Caroline herself—from what I've heard, she was a feisty woman, especially for Victorian times."

Annie couldn't help grinning. "You're right," she said. "Somehow Caroline managed to convince her proper Victorian father to finance her studies so that she could become an art historian. And later she really went to battle with her husband when she decided to turn their house into a museum—while they were still living in it. Poor Charles Darcy III met his match when he married Caroline."

Derrek studied her as she spoke. His gaze was intense and compelling, and it unsettled her, but she looked back at him purposefully.

"I still don't understand," she said. "If you don't really want to be a trustee, why not let the job go to someone else?"

"I have a responsibility," he said shortly. "As soon as I feel I've taken care of it, someone else can have all the aggravation."

"So you're only temporary."

"That's right." Derrek moved closer to her. "Does that bother you, Annie? Maybe you have plans about how you can influence the trustees to make you director of the museum. Maybe that's one of your projects—finding any method that will work for you. But you wouldn't want to waste your efforts on someone who isn't going to stick around."

"That's not true!" she said angrily, stepping back. Derrek continued to advance on her.

"There's nothing wrong with campaigning," he shot out at her. "Just as long as you do it the right way. Don't you agree with that, Annie?" His tone was dangerous. Annie backed herself into the barbed wire of the fence; as she made contact with it, her blouse snagged and suffered the same fate as her jacket.

"I don't believe in office politics," she declared, tilting her chin so she could glare at him. "All anyone has to do is look at my work record and read some of the proposals I've prepared. That's where the proof lies about my ability to handle the job."

He stood so close now, still gazing down at her with that speculative expression. "You almost convince me, Annie," he murmured. "Almost." He smiled at her, his black hair tousled over his forehead and his eyes an even deeper blue than before. His hand came up to brush, ever so lightly, against her cheek. She drew in her breath, but then he moved away from her.

"Come on, Annie," he said gently. "Come with me down the Turquoise Trail."

The words were seductive, promising adventures that Annie had never known or even dreamed. But she remained pressed against the barbed wire, feeling it almost prickle her flesh. Her heart was beating far too quickly. At the same time her head was warning her that if she were wise, she wouldn't go anywhere with Derrek F. Richards—not anywhere at all.

CHAPTER TWO

ANNIE SCRAMBLED into the Jeep without Derrek's help. She'd hiked her skirt unceremoniously above her knees, the kick pleat giving her the room she needed to maneuver. Derrek chuckled as he started the engine, but Annie pulled her skirt down with a sense of triumph. All her life she'd been finding solutions to problems that challenged her self-sufficiency and ingenuity. Derrek Richards was turning out to be one of those problems, but she would not allow him to get the better of her no matter how much he tried.

The road climbed into some hills, then dipped toward a scattering of buildings. Annie pulled the hair away from her face again and caught glimpses of crumbling adobe and weathered wood.

"This is the town of Golden," Derrek said. "It was much livelier during New Mexico's gold-rush days. But even then there was never enough water in these mountains. The prospectors actually had to melt snow so they could pan for gold, and they risked freezing to death in the winter. I can always picture them, their eyes burning with the hope of riches even while their fingers turned blue."

Annie shivered, the past calling out to her in this harsh and rugged land. She was always susceptible to the past; she had devoted her life to preserving its fragile legacies. But Derrek's voice truly made it come alive for her, as if all she had to do was reach out her hand and a time barrier would shatter at her touch.

She was pensive as the road climbed yet again, making its way through a mountain pass. As the Jeep mounted the ridge, the ground fell away to reveal a breathtaking view of more distant mountains across a valley. Down below were signs of another town, this one promising to be a bit larger than the last one.

"Is that Santa Fe?" Annie asked hopefully. Derrek shook his head, smiling.

"It's Madrid, an old coal-mining town."

The Jeep descended toward it. Annie looked at the dark tailings scarring the hillside, at the shacks buckling on their foundations, like old men about to fall to their knees. Derrek pulled the Jeep into a parking lot and turned to her.

"It's almost lunchtime," he said. "Are you hungry?"

"A little," Annie admitted. "But I think we should push on to Santa Fe."

"Eating is something useful," Derrek said in a deadpan voice. "It's an activity even you can approve of—as long as you don't enjoy your food too much."

Annie shot a glance at him. "I'm not as rigid as you think," she declared. "I know how to enjoy myself at the proper time."

Derrek laughed; it was a rich deep sound, coming easily as if he indulged in laughter often.

"You know what you need, Annie Brooke? You need to learn how to enjoy yourself at the improper time. I'm going to see if I can teach you that." His smile looked wicked. Annie slid down from the Jeep and smoothed out her skirt. All her instincts were on alert, warning her not to let down her guard around Derrek. She walked beside him with her usual brisk stride as they went along the narrow main street of Madrid.

The wooden houses here were substantial and yet engagingly shabby; some of them had been converted into shops. There was also a row of stores behind a planked walkway. Derrek escorted Annie up narrow wooden steps toward them, holding her arm. His fingers rubbed over the crisp rayon of her blouse, sending a tingling warmth right through to her skin. He dropped his hand just as she was about to pull away, and Annie had the distinct feeling that he was still laughing at her. She studied his grave expression suspiciously, not able to find even a quirk of a smile there. She didn't trust him; so far she had found him to be an unpredictable man. Her heels tapped firmly over the wooden planks as she preceded him into the store that proclaimed itself the Madrid Emporium.

The place was dim and cluttered inside, appearing to be a combination grocery store, restaurant and antique shop. On the windowsill a rusty lantern and a set of chipped plates were offered for sale, and Annie gravitated toward them. The plates were quite ordinary, worthless in spite of their exorbitant price, but the lantern had possibilities. Annie wondered if it had been used down in the mines. She bent to examine it more closely, listening absently as Derrek called for service.

"Hello—anybody home? Hello!" He sounded good-natured, not impatient even when no one answered after several calls. He propped one elbow on the counter, waiting, and eventually a rustle could be heard from the back of the store.

A slender elderly man with a face seamed like old wood came into view. He gazed at Derrek and Annie with a frowning perplexity—as if he rarely had customers and didn't really want to bother with them.

"Hello there," Derrek said. "Do you have a picnic basket? That's the first thing for a day like today."

"No," the man answered. He turned and began retreating to the back of the store.

"Make it a paper sack, then," Derrek called after him. The old man seemed to waver for a moment between coming forward and simply disappearing. At last he stepped toward Derrek and with an air of reluctance brought out a grocery sack.

"Let's see," Derrek said. "We'll need some cheese—cheddar and Swiss—some rolls, a bag of potato chips, a few apples and two bottles of root beer. Want anything else, Annie?"

Annie shook her head. She watched as the old man moved about slowly and precisely. It took a while, but Derrek's order was filled to exactness. The man frowned down at the money Derrek placed on the counter as if it was merely one more nuisance. Then he faded into the dimness at the back of the store.

Annie emerged into the sunlight. She followed Derrek across the street and through a stretch of weeds. They cut a path between two houses and went up a slope to cross a dirt road. By this time she knew better than to ask where they were going or why on earth they were going there.

Derrek led her to a tumbling old shack marked with a faded notice that said No Trespassing. Annie stopped, watching as Derrek settled himself on the porch.

"Didn't you read the sign?" she asked. He began rummaging in the grocery sack.

"Don't ever obey signs, Annie," he instructed her. "They'll just keep you out of places you want to be."

"You can't go around doing things like that," she protested. "Whenever I put up a sign at the museum, I expect it to be strictly obeyed. I believe in signs."

He pried open a roll and tucked two slices of cheese into it, one cheddar and one Swiss. He held it out to her.

"Learn to live dangerously," he said. "Break a rule now and then."

She stood her ground, ignoring the sandwich. "It says No Trespassing."

Derrek settled back more comfortably, stretching his long legs down the porch steps. He took a good-size bite of the roll.

"Suit yourself. This is my place, by the way. I'm the one who put up the sign."

Annie felt deflated and foolish. She stalked up the steps to sit beside him and grabbed her own roll. With surprise she realized how hungry she was, and she did justice to her share of the lunch. She bit into an apple and sipped her root beer. Boards creaked every time she shifted position. She glanced around. The shack had no door and the windows gaped crookedly. All the wood was so old that it had turned a silvered gray.

"This place is about to fall apart," Annie observed. "It's a shame, but I suppose it wasn't much of a house to begin with."

"You're right. It was cramped and drafty. The miner's family who lived here probably longed for one of the nicer places on Silk Stocking Row." Derrek gestured down toward the main street. "Those houses were only for the mining elite. You'll hear different stories about this town. Some people say that the workers were completely happy. The Christmas lights that blazed in Madrid every year were famous, a symbol of hope. But there are grim stories, too, about the rule of the company store, mine shafts that were far too dangerous, labor unions that never had a chance here."

Derrek's words seemed to hang in the air, transforming themselves into ghosts of another time. Annie could almost see the people who had once lived in this house—a man who was stooped from years in the mine shafts, a woman cooking yet another supper of beans in her small kitchen, the children who played in the dirt outside. Annie clasped her hands on her knees, her half-eaten apple forgotten.

"You can feel it, too, can't you?" Derrek asked softly. "You understand why I want to restore this shack."

Annie nodded slowly. "Yes, I understand," she murmured. "You're like me. You don't want the past to be forgotten or swept aside." Annie felt breathless, sitting here and sharing something this special with Derrek. It vibrated in the air, a connection between them even though they'd known each other only a short while. How could it be?

Annie stood up suddenly, alarmed at this emotional closeness.

"Would you like a tour of my mansion?" Derrek asked as he, too, rose to his feet. Annie's palms were damp with nervousness, and she rubbed them together surreptitiously. They stepped through the open doorway, and once again he guided her with a hand on her arm.

Sunlight filtered into the shack but could not dissipate the old and musty air. There was a toolbox in the corner, and fresh boards nailed onto one area of the floor. "Are you going to live here someday?" Annie asked. "It's awfully small, but somehow I think it would be right for you."

He grinned. "If nothing else, I'll come here when I need to get away from things. I do that already. I like working here, polishing up my carpentry skills."

"An architect and a carpenter," Annie mused. "That's a good combination."

"I'm glad you approve." His tone was light, but his face was serious as he gazed down at her. Annie could not look away from his eyes; right now they were so clear they seemed almost translucent. Then Derrek bent his head and gently kissed her.

His mouth was cool and firm, exploring the contour of her lips but making no demands. Annie was caught in stillness under his touch, the blood heating slowly in her veins. His lips moved over her cheek, to her temple where a pulse throbbed. She couldn't move, confused by her longing for another of his kisses. But even while she longed, she didn't know how to show him what she wanted.

He gazed down at her again, unsmiling. Perhaps he was thinking how unresponsive she was, how unsatisfactory. Her cheeks burned with embarrassment. She stepped back quickly, then gasped as her foot went through a rotting floorboard.

Derrek grabbed hold of her, his arms firm and strong around her.

"Steady," he murmured, edging her over to the door. "That was my fault. I should have warned you about the hazards in here."

Yes, there were dangers here, and Derrek posed the greatest of all. Annie felt so unsure with him. Now he made her lean against the doorjamb while he knelt to examine her foot.

"It's fine," she said. "I didn't hurt it at all." She tried to scoot away from him, but deftly he slipped off her shoe and probed for damage.

Annie flushed even more uncomfortably than before. Her stockings were practically in shreds after tramping through the weeds. She was totally disheveled, as if she'd starting coming apart at the seams the minute she met Derrek. Already he was more familiar with her feet than any man she had ever known.

"You seem to be all right," he pronounced. Annie slipped her foot back into her shoe with relief. She busied herself with the remains of their picnic, repacking everything neatly in the sack. Derrek said nothing about their kiss, looking relaxed as they headed back to the Jeep. Annie stuffed the grocery bag behind her seat, reflecting angrily that the encounter had probably meant nothing to him. So why was *she* getting so flustered over it?

They drove onward in silence and eventually the desert landscape flattened, stretching for miles. But always other mountains beckoned, hazy and blue in the distance. Annie began to see clusters of houses, and then a sign pointing the way to Santa Fe. Derrek bypassed the turnoff and kept right on driving.

"Wait!" Annie exclaimed. "Where are you going? The sign said we were supposed to turn."

"Remember, Annabel, you can't just go through life following signs."

He was maddening. Annie scowled at him, but he kept his eyes on the road. His shirtsleeves were rolled up carelessly, his hair whipped by the wind. He looked more rakish than ever. He fit so naturally into this land of desert and mountain, sun and clear sky. But it was also a land of mystery.

"We're in the foothills of the Sangre de Cristo Mountains now," Derrek said. Annie repeated the words to herself. Sangre de Cristo. It was more poetry, unfamiliar on her tongue. She noted how quickly the landscape had changed again, from sage to pine. Derrek swung off the highway onto a dirt road that climbed into the trees. Their branches reached out to brush against Annie, bringing with them the pungent perfume of the forest. The road took a turn, leveled out, and the Jeep came into a clearing.

The house was lovely—a low rambling adobe structure that looked as if it had been molded from the earth. Sunlight streamed through the trees, warming the adobe to a golden rose.

"Your destination at last," Derrek said to her. "You didn't have anything to worry about, after all. I was going to get you here sooner or later."

Annie's eyes followed the lines of the pleasing rounded walls; they went off at different angles as if the house could not decide where to end itself. Vines rambled up some of the walls, and wooden beams poked out along the tops of others. Annie had an urge to start exploring right away, convinced she would find all sorts of intriguing nooks and crannies. She made an effort to sound businesslike.

"I don't understand," she said. "I assumed I would be staying at a hotel In Santa Fe, and working in the Richards Foundation offices. But right now we're in the middle of nowhere." Even as she said that, she knew it wasn't true. She was most definitely in the middle of somewhere—somewhere peaceful and beautiful.

Derrek went around to the back of the Jeep to unload her boxes. "The painting you'll be restoring is here," he said, his voice strained again. "I didn't want it moved to the foundation office. It will be much more convenient if you stay here with me—otherwise you'll have to travel from Santa Fe every day. There's plenty of room for both of us."

Annie opened her mouth to protest, then closed it without saying anything. She didn't relish the thought of being alone here with Derrek, and yet the place drew her with its meandering grace and its simplicity. She slid down from the Jeep and went for her suitcase.

"You have a wonderful house," she said. "I envy you living in a place like this."

He gave a harsh laugh that held no humor. "I grew up here," he said. "I was glad to get away and not very happy to come back. But I'll be staying here until I have the foundation in order, along with the rest of my father's estate.''

Annie said nothing more, sensing the dark currents that ran in Derrek underneath his casual manner. It seemed this place was not so peaceful, after all. She followed him up the stone steps, waiting as he opened a carved wooden door.

Inside was incredible clutter—boxes strewn over wooden floors, stacks of books in the corners, piles of clothing heaped on the sofa.

"My father was a pack rat," Derrek explained, setting Annie's boxes down in one of the few empty spaces. "I've found suits he wore in the 1940s. Damned if I know what to do with them."

Annie wanted to ask more about Derrek's father, but something warned her to refrain. Gradually she was able to pick out details in all the chaos. The furniture was an odd mixture of antiques and junk; she saw a Queen Anne wing chair in superb condition alongside a bookshelf nailed together out of crates. Paintings lined almost every inch of the walls, and she recognized instantly which ones had been executed by Carlisle Richards. She was very familiar with his work, for the Darcy Museum had a whole wing dedicated to it. Now she went to stand before one of his paintings here. It depicted a vivid desert landscape of red earth and green scrub, done in his own unique style—bold colors and shapes against a flat background.

"He was good, wasn't he?" Derrek said dispassionately. "He maintained his originality while appealing to a broad range of people. A lot of that was shrewdness on his part. He wanted to make sure his paintings would be hanging in hundreds of living rooms, as well as in art galleries." There was something chilling in Derrek's words; he might have been speaking about a stranger, not his own father. Annie looked at the signature on the painting, a bold "Carlisle" scribbled in the lower right-hand corner. She herself had glimpsed Carlisle Richards only once or twice at the museum—a large flamboyant man with wavy gray hair. Derrek resembled him only faintly, and apparently the two men had not been close.

"I'll take you to your room," Derrek said, breaking the tense mood. He led her into a hall and around a corner. "Here it is. It's been used mainly for storage, but it's the cleanest one in the house." He sounded slightly apologetic. Annie stood in the doorway, surveying more chaos. Every available surface was covered with books, papers and knickknacks. Annie thought she saw a bed buried in there somewhere.

"It needs a little clearing out," Derrek admitted. "I'm still trying to sort through everything."

For a moment Annie was daunted. Right now all she craved was a quiet orderly retreat from Derrek. He caused such disturbing sensations inside her, and she needed to get them under control. But it seemed she would have to create her own sanctuary. With determination Annie unbuttoned the cuffs of her blouse and rolled up her sleeves. She liked to tackle a job right away and get it done. Grabbing a stack of books, she carted it out of the room. Derrek watched her with mocking amusement, then picked up a stack of books himself. They worked together in silence, passing each other in the doorway with arms full of old file folders, bags of newspapers, a whole set of pottery, four different pairs of candlesticks and always more books.

As the room grew bare its charm was revealed. It was larger than it had first appeared, with its own bathroom attached. A rounded fireplace graced one corner, and the windows were set deep in the thick adobe walls.

"All you need now is some furniture," Derrek said, and he disappeared abruptly. Annie stood beside her suitcase, hearing him make a fearful clatter and rattle in some other part of the house. Then there was silence, and a moment later he reappeared bearing an exquisite Louis XV table decorated with marquetry— delicate inlays of wood in a flower design. Annie stared at it.

"That's priceless," she breathed.

"It's your bedside table," he informed her, setting it down and disappearing again before she could protest. After a moment he dragged in an ordinary chest of drawers. Annie was relieved; here was something she didn't mind using. She began unpacking her suitcase, watching uneasily as Derrek transformed the room. Two Chippendale chairs, a small writing desk in fine old cherry, a Victorian fainting couch—

"Stop!" Annie cried in desperation, emerging from the closet. "It's all beautiful. It's *too* beautiful—I'll be afraid to move or even breathe in here."

"You've been around museums too long," Derrek chided. "This furniture was made for living. My mother collects this stuff, and she always intends it to be used."

"Your mother," Annie murmured, realizing that she'd never thought of Carlisle Richards as having a wife. "Does your mother live here, too?" Annie asked cautiously.

Derrek shook his head. "It's her house now, but after the—after my father's death, she felt that she had to leave. She's in Boston, living with her sister."

Annie's hand hovered over the writing desk with its intricate design of cubbyholes. It was such a work of craftsmanship that she could not bring herself to touch it.

"Your mother must have found it difficult to leave these antiques behind. I really can't use them, Derrek. You're right—I would know how to care for them in a museum, but that's all. I don't know how to live with things like this."

"I think they need to be used," Derrek said slowly. "My mother collected them during the years she was married to my father. It was the one thing she had for herself. Everything else..." He gave a shrug that seemed a gesture of defeat. "Just enjoy them—please. Here, look at these." He set a pitcher and a basin down on the bureau; they were made of lovely blue china. "They suit you, Annie. Some Victorian girl must have used them when she washed her face every morning. I can imagine you doing the same thing, wearing a white petticoat as you splash water onto your cheeks." He made the image sound very intimate. Annie fingered the handle of the pitcher, her skin suffusing with warmth.

"I'm afraid I'll vote for running water any day," she murmured. "At heart I'm a practical person."

Derrek leaned against the bureau, regarding her. "I don't think you know what you are at heart, Annie

Brooke. Maybe it's time for you to find out." His voice was low and thoughtful.

Annie tilted her chin. "I know exactly who I am," she said crisply. "And I'll allow these antiques in here only if you get me a bedside table I can really use. I'm not going to plunk my water glass down on that beautiful piece of marquetry. You can move it into a corner and I'll simply admire it."

Derrek chuckled, obliging her. He produced a table that was squat and ugly and entirely serviceable. Afterwards he unfolded a sheet and started smoothing it over the bed.

"I'll do that," Annie said quickly, taking one of the corners and snapping it around the edge of the mattress. Derrek just smiled at her, finishing his side and proceeding to unfold the top sheet. They ended up making the bed together, the sheet billowing between them and drifting down onto the mattress. Next came a soft Indian blanket patterned in earth tones. While Annie spread that out evenly, Derrek held a pillow under his chin and struggled to cram it into a case. Annie went to help him, laughing at his wild efforts. She took the pillow from him and neatly finished the job. Then she stood clutching it to her chest like a plate of armor as Derrek moved closer. His hand reached out to smooth her hair.

"We make a good team, Annie, don't you think?" He bent his head over hers. She stared at him, her throat dry. She could not allow him to kiss her again, to be disappointed in her.

"Derrek—please show me the painting I'm supposed to restore. I . . . it's time for me to begin work."

Her voice was shaky. As she mentioned the painting, a shadow crossed Derrek's face and he stepped back.

"Yes, I suppose it's time," he said. "I keep thinking the whole damned problem will go away, but it won't."

Annie released the pillow, placing it on the bed. She didn't know what emotions had spent themselves in this house, or what emotions still churned beneath the surface. She did not understand Derrek's pain, but she wished she could ease it for him somehow. The intensity of her wish startled her—she barely knew this man! And yet already he had touched her far too deeply.

Suddenly she was reluctant to see the painting, very reluctant. She followed Derrek silently down the hall to a closed door. He stood before it a moment, his fingers gripping the knob. Then, with a sharp angry movement, he twisted the knob and pushed open the door. He stood aside and Annie walked slowly into the room.

CHAPTER THREE

IT WAS A PORTRAIT painted by Carlisle Richards. It showed a man standing beside a seated woman, his hand resting on the back of her chair. This work, again, revealed the artist's distinctive style: color and pattern dominating, no sense of background depth. The real depth came from the expression on the woman's face. She was half-turned in her chair, her eyes on the man beside her. Her gaze held adoration, but uncertainty, too. She looked like a woman who was eager to please and yet afraid that she would be rejected in her efforts. What an artist Carlisle Richards had been to capture all that! Annie could not see the man's face in the portrait, for it had been obliterated. Paint had been slashed across it—an ugly smear of garish white. She clenched her hands in outrage. As Derrek brought her boxes of equipment into the room, she turned to him.

"This wasn't an accident," she declared. "Someone harmed this painting deliberately."

Derrek's face went cold and hard. "That's not your concern," he said. "All I want to know is if you can repair the damage."

It took all of Annie's self-control to turn back to the painting and give a reasoned response.

"Fortunately the damage isn't too extensive," she said tightly. "The portrait was varnished, which helped to protect it. I should be able to dissolve that smear of paint, or remove it a bit at a time."

"Good—I'll leave you to it, then." Derrek's manner was formal now as he walked to the door, but Annie could not contain herself any longer.

"Something like this shouldn't have happened!" she burst out. "A painting is...something special. I just don't understand how anybody could hurt one this way."

"Paintings can't feel," Derrek said, his voice rough. "People are what's important—or don't you believe that, Annie?"

She recoiled from the scorn in his voice.

"Of course I believe that," she said angrily. "I'm just trying to figure out what happened. I've seen canvases that got ripped when they fell down accidentally, or pictures that were burned in a fire and then doused with water. This painting has hardly suffered at all compared to those things. But it was damaged *intentionally*, and that's what makes me feel so...so furious." She wasn't going to back down, even though Derrek's eyes glinted dangerously.

He gestured at the painting. "You want to know the story, don't you, Annie? You want me to tell you exactly what happened so you'll have a logical explanation. Something neat and tidy to file away after you've been indignant long enough."

She shook her head. "I didn't mean it like that!" she protested. "I just want to understand."

His mouth twisted in a humorless smile. "It's not a story for you, Annie. It's not something you can clean up and put safely away in a museum. Everything safe and organized—that's the way you want life, isn't it? But it's not always like that. People and their emotions intrude all over the place. Just restore the painting, and don't ask any more questions about it.'' With that he left the room, pulling the door shut behind him.

Annie stared at the door, fury and hurt washing over her in waves. Derrek's words had cut her deeply, echoing what other people said about her. She wanted him to see her differently, but maybe that wasn't possible. Maybe everyone was right about her, after all. Maybe she lacked the vital and essential warmth to draw others to her. It was a desolate thought, and her mind veered quickly away from it.

At last Annie's heartbeat quieted, and she lifted her head. She would start working, for that always brought her solace. Going to her boxes, she knelt beside them and lifted the lids. This was like opening her own private treasure troves. Her equipment was arranged neatly inside the boxes: a portable gooseneck lamp, an assortment of cloths, brushes and cotton swabs, an array of solvents, an ultraviolet light, a pair of pliers, two screwdrivers, a magnifying glass and a jeweler's loupe, several gleaming scalpels . . .

It was a varied and intricate collection of tools. Gazing at it with pride, Annie felt the familiar sense of contentment. All that mattered now was the job at hand. She reached inside her yellow-and-green box, bringing out four padded blocks of wood. She had made the pads herself, with cotton batting and lengths of corduroy tacked snugly to the wood. The corduroy was a bright cheery red. Annie loved bold and vivid shades of color; she had decided long ago that she didn't have the right looks to wear bright colors, but she tried to give her life touches of them whenever possible.

Now she hummed under her breath as she went over to the painting. It was propped up on a table against the wall, a precarious position. Very carefully Annie took charge of it. She turned the painting face down, using her padded blocks to support each corner. With a screwdriver and pliers, she gently pried out the nails that held the painting in its frame. Annie had to call on many different skills in her work; sometimes she felt like a carpenter, sometimes like an artist or a surgeon. But always she had to move with meticulous care. It took her a long while to unframe the painting without causing it any harm. Again her blood pumped angrily as she thought about the damage inflicted so willfully here. She turned the portrait over, resting it on a clean sheet of glassine. Gazing down at the man and woman in the painting, she wondered who they could be. There was something familiar about the woman, something about the long graceful lines of her body and the deep blue of her eyes.

Derrek had eyes just that color and shape. Perhaps this was a portrait of his parents, and therefore a self-portrait of Carlisle Richards. Except that someone had deliberately defaced it.

Annie shivered, although the room wasn't cold. She made herself concentrate only on technical details, conducting a thorough examination of the painting to check for any other damage. As she became more involved, she lost track of the time. Often when she worked on a painting she would plug in a pot of coffee and keep herself going all day and night. The work was invariably tedious and painstaking, but even so she could be swept away by it.

Twilight had started to descend when Derrek returned. Annie straightened, magnifying glass in hand, wincing at the crick in her back. She snapped off her portable lamp, allowing shadows to creep over the room. Then she stood against the table, gazing warily at Derrek. He had changed into dark slacks and a grayish-blue shirt; now Annie realized what a natural elegance he had. He looked at the painting lying flat on the table.

"You haven't even started yet," he said with surprise. She stiffened.

"I've been working very hard," she informed him. "I've made a thorough analysis of the painting's condition. So far it seems to be structurally sound, no cracks or ruptures. But of course I'll make an examination with ultraviolet—"

"Forget all that," he said impatiently. "Can't you just get on with the job?"

"That's exactly what I'm doing," she retorted. Her temper flared, but from long practice she managed to control it. She lined up the index cards on which she'd laboriously copied all her facts and details, and then she moved to the window. "If I'd really wanted to do the job right, I would have cleaned up this room first. Look at all that dust in the air. That's bad for a painting."

Derrek came to stand beside her and peered at the dust motes that drifted about in the waning daylight.

"How beautiful they are," he murmured. "Like specks of gold or silver. But to you they're just dirt messing up the room."

"You think you know all about me, don't you?" she shot back. "But you're wrong—you don't know anything at all. Stop trying to judge me!" She turned away from him, but he caught hold of her hand.

"Listen, Annie," he began, "I'm sorry I growled at you earlier. I was using you as a scapegoat for my own frustrations. It wasn't fair." His fingers tightened on hers. "A lot of things have happened over the years in this house, and for me they're all symbolized by that damn painting. It tends to make me a little edgy."

Annie hesitated. "It's a portrait of your parents, isn't it?" she asked after a moment.

"Yes." He stated the word simply, offering her nothing more. Other questions bubbled inside Annie, but she didn't know how to push through Derrek's restraint to ask them. All she could do was go on standing next to him at the window. A silence stretched between them, taut and uncomfortable as if they were leaving too much unspoken. The golden dust motes began to fade as dusk deepened in the room. It was Annie who finally broke the silence, pulling her hand away from Derrek's.

"I'd better do some more work now," she said.

"I cooked dinner for you," he answered gravely. "You're going to have to stop now and eat it no matter how bad it tastes."

"All right, I'll take the risk." She chanced a small hesitant smile. "Just give me a few minutes to clean up." Derrek's presence was unsettling Annie all over again, and she retreated gratefully to her room down the hall. It was an attractive and welcoming place now, with its hodgepodge of antiques.

Annie stared at herself in the bathroom mirror, dismayed at the change that had taken place since she'd left the hotel in Albuquerque. Her hair had come loose from its elastic band and hung in unruly clumps, her cheeks were flushed and her lipstick had rubbed off. Her full lips, with their natural tint of deep coral, were parted breathlessly as if waiting for another of Derrek's kisses.

Annie set about putting her appearance to rights. She made her hair obey again, curling it under with her brush. She changed into crisp twill pants in her standard shade of navy, and chose a pale yellow blouse to go with them. Her lipstick went on firmly, with expert strokes to thin the contours of her mouth. She looked at herself critically.

Well, she'd managed to batten down the hatches, subdue her image once more. But suddenly that didn't seem satisfactory. Annie grabbed a tissue and rubbed the lipstick from her mouth. Now her lips were a darker pink than ever, lush and inviting. Recklessly she allowed them to stay that way. She couldn't delay much longer: Derrek was waiting for her with dinner. Annie went out to the hall and without too much trouble found the dining room.

She bumped against a packing crate, but Derrek had done a good job of disguising most of the clutter in here. The only light came from candles flickering in ornate silver candelabra, and this made all the piles of junk fade into the shadows. Annie smiled at this stratagem, but getting to the table was like traversing a mine field. She felt her way along cautiously, sliding into a chair just as Derrek pushed through a swinging door from the kitchen. He was bearing a gigantic salad bowl.

Annie had expected something uninspired like hamburgers and frozen French fries tossed into a skillet. Instead Derrek served her a broiled salmon steak, vegetables in herb sauce and slices of warm French bread. The salad was the most impressive fare of all, an exuberant mixture of endive lettuce, tomatoes, sunflower seeds, cabbage, diced apples and raisins.

"This is wonderful," Annie said, spearing a raisin with her fork. "And it's definitely original."

"I think I put two salads together by accident," Derrek remarked, pouring Annie some chilled water into a wine goblet. He had an ability to take something mundane and transform it into something far from ordinary—even the water, which sparkled through myriad prisms in the goblet. Annie took a long sip of it.

They were sitting at a table of heavy dark wood, carved in a Spanish style. The chairs had high massive backs like thrones, but they were surprisingly comfortable. Annie leaned her head back, watching the play of candlelight. It heightened the bold angles and planes of Derrek's face as he settled back in his own chair.

"You've spent all your life at that museum, Annie Brooke," he murmured. "Don't you ever want to try something different?"

She shook her head. "My work there is always different. I get to travel, and every day I seem to learn something new. But it's more than that. Sometimes I

like to imagine that I'm carrying on for Caroline
Darcy herself. She loved art, and she wanted to share
it with everyone. She wanted her house to be the kind
of museum anyone could wander into."

"Anyone...like a young girl searching for a home,"
Derrek said softly. Annie picked up her fork of heavy
sterling, balancing it. For some reason it seemed important to make Derrek understand how much the
museum meant to her. But she'd never explained this
to anyone before, and so it was difficult to choose the
right words.

"The whole time I was growing up I never felt like
I had a real home," she said at last. "It wasn't just
because my parents divorced when I was seven. It's
what happened afterward. My father moved away
from Colorado, and my mother..." Annie set her fork
down with a little clatter. "She was so apathetic after
the divorce. She latched on to a really dead-end job,
and that was it. Nothing else. No spirit, no struggle for
something better. Every afternoon she just plodded to
work, and late every night she plodded back."

Derrek leaned forward now, propping his elbows on
the table. "That didn't give you much time with her,"
he observed.

Annie nodded. The words were coming to her more
easily now, as if she were exercising a long-forgotten
muscle.

"I hardly ever saw my mother," she said. "On her
days off she was so tired that she would just huddle in
a chair with a magazine. Our apartment was always so
quiet. Too quiet. I hated going home after school,
knowing I had all those hours ahead by myself.
Sometimes I tried making my own noise—turning up

the radio extra loud until the neighbors next door banged on the wall. But I liked knowing that someone else was in the building and could hear me. And then I found the museum. I didn't feel nearly so alone after that.''

"What about friends?" Derrek asked.

Annie smiled musingly. "I had a best friend named Colleen until seventh grade," she said. "But Colleen moved away and I found out that I didn't know the rules of being a teenager."

"Nobody knows the rules," Derrek said with a wry grin. "We all just muddle through somehow."

Annie traced a finger over the embossed pattern on her napkin. Talking to Derrek made her feel as if she hadn't really been so awkward and out of place as a teenager. She glanced over at him, enjoying the casual and easy atmosphere he seemed to know how to create.

"I hope you're ready for dessert," he said. "It's something I built myself, from the bottom up." He brought two bowls from the kitchen. They were made of exquisite cut glass, as fine as the china on which he'd served dinner. In each bowl was a creamy square of custard with a generous layer of caramel sugar.

"This is New Mexican flan," he said, waiting for her to taste it. Annie lifted her spoon, about to take a healthy bite in her usual matter-of-fact way, but the expectant look on Derrek's face called for something more. She dipped into the custard and put the portion delicately into her mouth, where she savored it for a moment; it melted smoothly and richly on her tongue, and she could taste just the right hint of vanilla. She closed her eyes, allowing a smile of satisfaction to play over her face.

"Mmm..." She sighed at the tang of caramel. When she opened her eyes, she knew from Derrek's pleased expression that she had properly conveyed her approval. She ate the rest of the flan in appreciative silence. Derrek was truly a good cook, a talent she herself had never developed.

"Annie, tell me something," Derrek said after he had finished his own custard. "Why not let Vance Forester take over as director of the museum, and you can step in as assistant director? That way you'd have some of the power you want."

At the mention of Vance's name, Annie tensed inside. "That wouldn't do at all," she said emphatically. "Vance and I just don't have the same ideas. We'd always be at odds if we had to work that closely together."

Derrek looked at her thoughtfully. "You really don't like Vance, do you?" he asked.

That was an understatement, but Annie tried not to expose her personal reasons for disliking Vance. "He and I agree on only one thing," she said. "We both realize the museum is stagnating. Vance has a solution—he wants to sell the Darcy house and construct a new building in a wealthy neighborhood. He keeps talking about 'brushing up our image.' But moving like that is the last thing we should do! The spirit would be entirely lost. We'd be the Caroline Darcy Museum in name only. And we'd be much less accessible to the lower-income people who really need us."

"Tell me about your own plan, Annie. I can see you have one." Derrek sounded genuinely interested, but she didn't need any encouragement on this subject. She gripped the stem of her goblet.

"Right now the museum is in a perfect location," she declared. "Behind us there's an empty lot, and beyond that an old woolen mill that's been shut down for years. It's really an historic building in its own right." Annie gazed at Derrek, wanting very much to share her vision with him. Words alone didn't seem enough, so she picked up her fork and used it to gesture enthusiastically. "Now, I propose that we buy up the empty lot behind us, as well as the mill, and we create a whole museum center. The empty lot will become a park, and of course the Caroline Darcy house will continue as the main building for the museum. And the mill..." Annie couldn't repress her excitement, and all her ideas began to tumble out.

"Oh, the mill, Derrek! It has so many possibilities. It's big enough to handle some of the new displays I have in mind. An exhibit on trains, or the history of flight—the kind of thing that will really appeal to kids. We'll even have an exhibit that traces the history of the mill itself, something that'll tell the story of the children and women who used to work there under such difficult conditions. You see, we need to be more than an art museum, Derrek, much more than that!" She waved her fork so ardently that she nearly jabbed his arm. He shifted to a safer distance.

"We should be much more involved in education," she raced on. "We should be collaborating with schools all the time. I want to have a special place to display children's art. Oh, and art classes for both kids and adults. We could set up some large classrooms in the mill building. And we'd need a van that would travel around to the schools. We could call it the Museum Mobile and it would have all sorts of fun things inside, like fossils and arrowheads and old maps." Annie stopped, knowing her enthusiasm was getting ahead of her. But she longed so intensely to use her ideas, to fulfill her vision for the museum.

Derrek rubbed his jaw. "What kind of shape is this mill building in?" he asked.

"It's in very good condition for its age." Annie tried to be more restrained now. "Of course, extensive remodeling will have to be done, but it won't cost nearly as much as constructing a new building. Can't you just see it, Derrek? The park in the middle, bringing it all together. Well . . . what do you think?"

"I like it," he said. "And I liked the way you talked about it. I enjoyed seeing you loosen up a little. Your eyes are sparkling right now, Annie. You know, I still don't have you figured out," Derrek went on slowly, watching her. "Sometimes you're so full of fire and passion, but other times you sound almost clinical. All day I've been trying to decide what you're really like."

Annie flushed, and tried to shield herself from his probing.

"I'm not that difficult to understand," she said. "I know where I want to go with my life, and I'm just trying to get there as best as I can. I have a direction. What more do you need to know?"

"I'm curious about you. Maybe you should take that as a compliment. You're a very beautiful woman, Annie, and I can't help wanting to know more about you."

His words were like a caress. Annie had never considered herself beautiful. Nor had she spent a great deal of time worrying about her looks; she'd always accepted them for what they were—passable. But Derrek was forcing her to look at herself in a new way.

Now Derrek rose from his chair and disappeared into the shadows. Annie heard a clattering noise—his foot must have struck something—and then a moment later soft music drifted into the room. It was a ballad, poignant and beautiful to Annie although sung in a language she didn't understand. Derrek came back, holding out his hand to her, and she stood up uncertainly. He drew her close and whirled her about. She gasped in surprise, clinging to him.

"I don't know how to dance," she protested. Derrek chuckled against her temple.

"You're doing just fine," he reassured her. "I think you have a natural aptitude."

He made another turn, taking Annie around the table. She pivoted with him, and his talent alone kept her from trampling his feet. But now they'd ended up in a corner where there was simply no room to maneuver; they were surrounded by more packing crates and stacks of newspapers.

Derrek drew Annie closer, moving her back and forth in small steps. Her breath came unsteadily at his nearness. His body was lean and hard next to hers, and yet it yielded to her, accommodating her softer curves. Annie pressed her cheek against Derrek's chest, feeling the strong beat of his heart. Its steady rhythm hardly seemed fair when her own pulse was jumping about so erratically. Derrek's arms around her, the slow plaintive music, the flickering candle-light—all combined to intoxicate Annie more than any wine Derrek could have poured into her goblet. She stiffened her body, torn between longing and fear.

"Derrek..."

"Yes?" he murmured against her hair, then hummed gently with the music.

"Derrek, I'm glad you like my ideas for the museum," she burst out, desperate to put things on a business level. "If I could just become director..."

Derrek drew back from her, looking down into her face. She was grateful that the light of the candles reached them only faintly. She didn't want him to read any of her turbulent emotions.

"Is it always the museum for you, Annie? Does that come before everything else?" he asked.

"Yes, it does," she said. That was the truth—her work came first. It was the one thing she'd always been able to count on.

"So you'll do anything to reach your goal, to be director of the place." His tone was blunt. Annie stared up at him, but the darkness that protected her also cloaked him, and she could not study his expression.

"I'll do whatever it takes to get that job and keep it," she answered steadily and proudly.

"Even this, Annie Brooke?" he asked softly. "Would you do even this?" He pulled her close again and captured her mouth with his. At first Annie melted against him, her mouth pliant under his. But this was not like the first gentle kiss he had given her in the old mining shack. Now his lips ruthlessly demanded more, taunting her even as they led her into delight. And through the thick beating of her pulse, his harsh challenge echoed back to her. *Even this, Annie Brooke? Would you do even this?*

She struggled out of his arms, her breathing ragged.

"What are you trying to do?" she demanded, her voice shaking.

"I thought it was pretty clear," he said quietly. "I'm trying to find out just how far you'll go for that job you want so much. I *am* one of the trustees—you'll need my vote. Exactly what will you do to get it?"

She felt sickened by his calculated attempt at seduction. What a fool she'd been! She had opened herself up to him, lulled by candlelight and good food and his false warmth. All along he had wanted only to see what price she was willing to pay for her dreams.

Annie stared back at him in defiance, even as the sickness churned inside her. When she spoke, her voice was icy and perfectly under control.

"I don't give a damn if you *are* a museum trustee. I don't care if you could hand over that job to me right now. Just stay away from me. Don't ever touch me again." Then she turned and walked calmly to her room, giving no sign of the trembling deep inside her. Even in the darkness and the clutter she did not stumble once.

CHAPTER FOUR

ANNIE CLOSED and locked the door to her room, then sat down carefully on the bed. The trembling spread out from her stomach until she had to wrap her arms tightly around herself. She didn't want to think about anything at all, and yet her mind followed its own cruel logic, replaying over and over the humiliating scene with Derrek. How could she have trusted him? She had started to awaken at his touch, and yet it had all been a terrible mistake.

A knock sounded at the door.

"Annie, we need to talk," Derrek said from the other side. She didn't answer, for she'd already said everything that needed saying. In the morning she would leave this house, and Derrek could find someone else to restore the painting.

"Annie, at least you owe me the chance to explain myself to you," Derrek said. "I do have an explanation."

She didn't want to hear it. Too many new emotions had battered her today, leaving her completely drained. But Derrek would not give up.

"I'll be in the kitchen, Annie, waiting for you." She heard his footsteps receding down the hall. For a long moment she stayed frozen in place. She didn't have any reason to listen to him, and she couldn't think of anything less appealing than going out there to confront him again. Yet part of her wanted very badly to believe in him. She finally rose from the bed, unlocked the door and made her way to the kitchen.

It was a disaster area—pots, pans and plates from their dinner strewn about with wild abandon. Several mixing bowls littered the counter, along with a whole collection of dirty spoons and knives. Derrek presided in the midst of all this, a kitchen towel tucked into his waistband. He was tossing dishes into a sink that billowed alarmingly with soap suds.

He turned when she came into the room. "I owe you an apology," he said. "Please. Sit down and hear me out."

She remained standing. "Go ahead—I'm listening," she answered curtly.

"I can understand why you're angry." Derrek raked a sudsy hand through his hair, leaving a wet trail. "I misjudged you," he said. "I believed what Vance Forester told me about you."

Annie pressed her hand against a countertop. "Exactly what did Vance say about me?" she asked coldly.

"It's not so much what he said, it's what he implied. But the meaning was clear—that you'd do anything you had to in order to be director of the museum—even if that meant sleeping with a trustee."

The anger inside Annie was white hot. She gripped the counter harder. "And you believed what he said." Her voice was shaking. "You actually believed I could be that calculating."

Derrek came to stand on the other side of the counter. "Listen to me, Annie. Just let me explain. The whole time I've been running this blasted foundation,

I keep coming up against people trying to use me—my name, my influence. That made it easy for me to believe Forester. After talking to him, I decided I was going to trap you at your own game. Believe it or not, I wasn't looking forward to it. You were just one more offensive detail I had to clear up in the morass of my father's estate. Then you pulled off your sunglasses and looked at me with those big dark eyes. Right away I started to doubt what Forester had said...and it seemed very important to find out the truth.''

"Is this supposed to make me feel better?" Annie asked rigidly. "You've been testing me all day. When you kissed me in the shack, that's what you were doing."

"All right, yes, maybe I was testing you, but it was more than that. I wanted to kiss you, Annie. My instincts kept telling me that Forester was wrong about you. But tonight when I was holding you in my arms—lord, you sounded like you really *would* do anything to get that job."

"You just assumed that!" Annie exclaimed. "You didn't give me a chance! You'd already written the script."

"Look, I'm trying to apologize. I'm saying I was wrong. I should have listened to what my instincts were telling me. The fact is, you're the kind of person who can't even disobey a No Trespassing sign."

Annie clenched her hands. "And now I'm supposed to tell you how grateful I am to have your stamp of approval. You've decided that I'm pure and morally upright."

"Yes, I have decided that. You're exactly the opposite of what Forester implied. You have no experience with men at all."

Annie hadn't thought it possible to be any angrier, but she was. She picked up a ladle and clutched it fiercely. There was dried herb sauce even on the handle.

"My private life is no concern of yours," she said tensely. "I came here to restore a painting, and that's all. When I think about what you did to me tonight... Just tell me this, Derrek. Exactly what would you have done if I'd been eager to pay a price for your vote? Just how far would you have allowed me to go?"

Derrek's eyes glittered as he leaned across the counter. "Now you should listen to your own instincts, Annie Brooke. Aren't they telling you what I would have done?"

She gazed back at him, then sighed. "They're sending me a message, loud and clear. They're telling me that you would have kicked me out of your house before I so much as undid an earring."

"You're not wearing earrings," Derrek observed thoughtfully, "but you do understand how I feel about people who try to use me." He relaxed his stance and rested his arms on the counter. "Annie, a lot of people see that I'm Carlisle Richards's son, and that's all they see. So this morning I expected to go down to Albuquerque and find some bouncy twit of a girl ready to ooze all over me."

"Bouncy twit?" Annie echoed in disbelief. "That's how Vance described me?" She put the ladle down and wiped her sticky hand with a dishcloth. Then she sank onto a stool at the counter. "I might as well tell you," she said tiredly. "Vance and I went out together for a while. The experience was pretty awful. He just wanted something physical—and I didn't want *him* at all. I bruised his ego, but this revenge of his is really vicious." She felt sick again, thinking about it. Derrek poured two mugs of coffee from a freshly brewed pot and pushed one over to her. She took it, although it wouldn't do her jangled nerves any good. Derrek sat across from her, sipping his own coffee reflectively.

"I'm sorry I was part of his revenge. I wish I hadn't been, Annie."

She wrapped her hands around her mug and stared into it. She hadn't told Derrek what Vance had finally said to her. She remembered it all perfectly, and now it reverberated in her mind: "You're cold and frigid, Annie. You don't know how to please a man, and maybe you never will. Maybe your heart only beats when you see a man painted on canvas. . . ."

It wasn't true! Her heart had started beating at a new and unfamiliar tempo the first time she'd looked into Derrek's blue eyes. Vance had never made her feel this way; no man had ever made her feel this way. And yet Vance had still voiced her greatest fear. If she ever found a man who touched her heart, would she be able to make him happy at all?

She didn't know the answer to that question. All she could do was go on sitting here across from Derrek, feeling the warmth he gave her. She knew only that in one day under the bright New Mexico sun, her life had started to change irrevocably.

WHEN ANNIE EMERGED from her room the next morning, she was relieved to find that Derrek had already left the house. She was still shaken after last night. Poking her head into the kitchen, she saw that it was now tidy. Yet Derrek had left his mark—dishcloths were tossed recklessly over the water spout, and pans were piled so precariously in the drainer that they looked as if they'd come crashing down at any minute. A bowl and a spoon were laid out on the counter, along with a box of cereal and a single daffodil stuck into a jar of water. Annie moved closer and saw a sheet of paper propped up against the jar. Bold handwriting was scrawled across it:

Annie Brooke, you have permission to trespass in this kitchen and eat an unlimited amount of breakfast.

A smile tugged at Annie's mouth. She opened the refrigerator door and thoroughly perused the contents. A loaf of sprouted-grain bread, several cartons of gourmet yogurt, a jar of strawberry preserves, two large eggplants and a container of leftover spaghetti. Annie found a quart of milk, deciding she would have just a bowl of cereal. She ate at the counter, gazing the whole time at her daffodil. It made her happy to think Derrek had left it for her.

When she'd finished eating, she washed and dried her bowl, making sure she hadn't left any mess behind. That was something else she'd learned as a child—to clean up all traces of herself. Her mother had never noticed when she did leave a mess, and eventually Annie had started cleaning up after herself

without being told. Nothing was lonelier than an un-
acknowledged mess.

Now Annie took the daffodil with her, setting it on
a shelf in her workroom. The painting waited for her
on the table, and she stood staring down at it for a
long moment. Carlisle Richards had used vibrant
colors to depict himself, but his wife was portrayed in
muted shades of lavender. She looked very beautiful,
but she faded out next to Carlisle's large broad-
shouldered body. Annie thought of Derrek; his own
frame was lean and rangy, not husky as his father's
had been. She wondered if the two men had had anything in common at all.

Annie had been thinking about Derrek ever since
she'd opened her eyes this morning. All her life she'd
taught herself to proceed with slowness and caution.
But something about Derrek made her feel reckless—
frightened and exhilarated at the same time. She had
to draw back, find out logically what was happening
to her. And yet logic seemed to be escaping her at the
moment. Even though Derrek wasn't near her right
now, he made her feel completely befuddled.

Annie turned to her work, determined not to think
about him anymore. She pulled the heavy curtains
across the window, blocking out the light so she could
examine the painting under ultraviolet. When she
switched the lamp on, that gash of paint over Carlisle's face leapt out at her with a purple glow. It had
been smeared on with a bold but shortened stroke, as
if an act of anger had been arrested even as it began.
The room's darkness pressed down on Annie, her focus that one angry streak. It was too vivid now, too
blatant. The ultraviolet rays seemed capable of ex-

posing not only coats of varnish and paint, but also the hidden emotions behind that violent act. Annie forced herself to finish examining the rest of the portrait. It appeared to be in good condition.

She was glad to pull open the curtains and have sunlight wash into the room. Everything seemed ordinary again. Taking her jeweler's loupe and a scalpel, Annie bent over the portrait to begin the delicate task of scraping away the gash of white paint.

She worked straight through lunch and on into the afternoon. But at last she had to stop for a break, for all her muscles were cramped and her stomach was demanding food. She ate a quick sandwich in the kitchen, and then wandered through the house. She'd been longing to explore this place.

Hallways rambled in all directions, with dark wooden floors and whitewashed walls. Overhead were thick exposed beams. Now and then Annie came upon small alcoves carved into the wall, where intricate wooden sculptures resided. She peered into rooms as she went, seeing everywhere a jumble of confusion. Pausing in one arched doorway, she saw a drafting table set up. She moved closer and examined the large sheet of paper clipped to the table. It was a house plan in progress, pencils and a T square waiting to continue the job. Annie surveyed the rest of the room. The walls were hung with weavings in striking geometric designs. A rumpled bed was set in the middle of the floor, a pair of scuffed cowboy boots sprawled beside it. Suddenly Annie felt like an intruder. This was Derrek's territory, and she didn't belong here. She left hastily, finding a back door that led outside. Here she could breathe the cool pine-scented air and exercise her sore muscles. She wandered along a brick path, an unkempt garden stretching on each side of her. Bulbs—including a few daffodils—had struggled up valiantly through the weeds. Annie smiled and walked on.

The trees thickened about her, the brick path disappearing into damp earth. Annie hesitated, then glimpsed an adobe wall ahead of her. She walked toward it, intrigued, and came to another clearing. In the center was a small guest house surrounded by its own garden wall. Annie leaned over the gate and saw that weeds had truly taken over here. Withered vines clung to a trellis, and scraggly bushes hugged the sides of the small house as if to protect it. Annie could not resist unlatching the gate and going to the door to see if it was locked. It wasn't, although the knob was stiff under her fingers and wouldn't turn at first. After a few jiggles she was able to push open the door. She stood on the threshold and saw a large desk, some easels and several paintings propped against the walls.

Annie knew that she had stumbled upon the studio of Carlisle Richards, and she let her breath out slowly. There was something so mournful about the abandoned paintings. A few of them were Southwestern landscapes; one showed a hawk in flight; another was a stark portrait of an Indian man. Yet they were all unfinished, as if Carlisle had lost interest halfway through each one and had turned to something new. That was sad, and at the same time eerie. Annie stood in the doorway, lost in her contemplation of the paintings. But then she heard the click of the gate behind her and she twisted around. Derrek came toward her; today he was wearing a jacket and a tie with his jeans. His jet-black eyebrows drew together in a frown.

"This isn't a good place to be, Annie," he said brusquely. She rubbed the gooseflesh that prickled along her arms.

"I'm sorry," she answered. "You're right, I shouldn't be here."

He brushed past her, stepping inside the studio and glancing around. "Nothing's changed," he muttered. "I don't know why I keep hoping it will." He stood motionless for a moment, then went on in a low voice, "I haven't been out here for a long while. I've been putting it off—making a decision about what to do with all this. Before my father died, he told my mother he wanted these paintings destroyed. She couldn't do it, and now it's left up to me."

Annie didn't say anything. Her first impulse was to cry out against destruction of the paintings, but there was so much she didn't understand. She could only watch as Derrek paced restlessly about the studio.

"When I was a kid, I never came out here," he said. "My mother made sure I stayed away when my father was working. Sometimes he'd sleep here, and we wouldn't see him for days. My mother would bring food to him, but she'd leave it outside the door on a tray. Later she'd go back and pick up the empty dishes. It was almost like we were keeping a prisoner here—but she was the real prisoner." Derrek looked up and gave a mirthless smile. "Should I stop, Annie? I don't want to destroy any illusions you have about the great Carlisle Richards."

Annie shifted uneasily in the doorway. "I've always admired his work," she said. "He seemed like someone special. Someone larger than life, I suppose."

"He would have relished hearing you say that," Derrek said, pausing before the painting of the hawk. His voice was careful, without emotion, as he continued. "My father spent a lot of money and effort to create his own legend. He set up the foundation to perpetuate himself; we have the Carlisle Richards scholarship, the Richards wing at your museum, the Carlisle awards for high-school students. None of those things would exist if my father hadn't been able to put his name on them."

It all sounded so cynical, and Annie had to protest. "He was such a great artist. That alone will make his name live on, won't it? Surely knowing that was enough for him."

Derrek shook his head. "Not for my father. He had to cover all the angles, because secretly he was terrified that he wasn't a great artist. He wanted to make sure he'd always be remembered for something." Derrek sat down behind the desk, and Annie saw the lines of tiredness etched into his face. He pulled his tie loose as if it had been choking him. "Right now I'm trying to run the foundation exactly the way it was set up," he said. "I spend all my time perpetuating my father's image, no matter how hard it is for me. But I'm tearing down that image right in front of you. Why should you be the one person given the dubious privilege of learning what Carlisle Richards was really like? Tell me that."

Annie was surprised to find that she had an answer for him. "Maybe it's because you know you can trust me," she said.

There was a spark of amusement in Derrek's expression, and a tenderness that seemed meant for her.

"Loyal, trustworthy Annie Brooke," he murmured. "That description fits you, all right. Lord, it feels good to talk to you—to let down the front for a little while."

"You must be a pretty loyal person yourself," Annie answered, "to keep up a front that goes against everything you feel."

Derrek made a wry grimace. "I'm not doing it for my father. It's what my mother needs right now. Her whole life has been dedicated to building the legend of Carlisle Richards."

"But you said she was a prisoner," Annie pointed out.

"She was a willing one. She worshiped my father, even when he abused her. It wasn't physical abuse—nothing like that. No, it was all emotional. Whenever she voiced an opinion, he always managed to belittle her. He did it so effectively that she never even knew what was happening to her—she just stopped believing in herself. My father couldn't allow anyone to share the spotlight with him. That would have been too risky." Derrek's voice was still carefully devoid of emotion, but Annie could see the pain in his eyes. She nodded slowly at his words, a shock of recognition coming to her.

"It's in the portrait," she said. "Your mother's in the background even though, technically speaking, there *is* no background in your father's paintings. But he managed it with her."

"He was a good artist, all right. Carlisle Richards could inflict the most subtle suffering, and then he could capture it on canvas. That takes a certain genius." There was no irony in Derrek's tone. He seemed to be stating a fact, nothing more. Annie rubbed her arms again and looked at the cobwebs gathering in the corners of the windows.

"Derrek . . . where did you fit in?" she asked. "Did your father . . . did he hurt you, as well?"

"I was stronger than my mother," he answered. "I fought back whenever he tried to put me down. We had some pretty bad shouting matches until I saw what that was doing to my mother. She wanted peace—not so much for herself, but for my father. She needed to protect him, and at last I understood that. I knew I'd always be an outsider with both my parents."

Annie understood that feeling of being outside. Growing up, she'd experienced it herself, in her own family. And she still felt like an outsider much of the time around other people. Derrek picked up an artist's brush from the top of the desk and turned it around in his fingers.

"I moved away from here as soon as I could," he told her. "I was happy with my life after that. I studied architecture, and after a few years I set up my own office in Albuquerque. Then my father died, and my mother couldn't handle anything. She ran as far as she could go—to her sister in Boston. And I came back here to pick up all the pieces Carlisle Richards left behind.''

His words sent a disturbing current through the air and Annie could no longer remain still. She stepped toward Derrek.

''No, Annie—don't come any closer,'' he said, and now the lines in his face seemed deeper. ''My father was a troubled person, and I can still feel that too strongly in this room. I don't want you to feel it, too.''

Annie withdrew, stepping back over the threshold. Derrek came to stand across from her, gazing down at her intently.

''I've had a hell of a time the last few months,'' he said. ''But one good thing has happened because of it all—yesterday I met you, Annie. Things are starting to look better.''

Annie felt touched by his words. She gazed back steadily at him as he went on.

''I have to get away from this place for a while,'' he said, ''away from the bitterness. Come with me, Annie.''

''Where will you take me?'' she asked.

''It doesn't matter. Anywhere. Just come with me. We'll have at least a few hours together, away from all the problems in our lives.''

She turned and stared at the weeds threatening to take over the path. Derrek had destroyed some of her illusions today; her admiration for Carlisle Richards was tainted now. Perhaps none of her illusions about life was safe with Derrek.

And yet she found herself turning back to him. The pull he exerted on her was too powerful. She needed to be with him right now. The need frightened her, but she couldn't resist it.

"Yes," she murmured, looking up at him. "Yes, I'll go with you."

CHAPTER FIVE

DERREK'S MOOD seemed to lighten with every mile the Jeep put between them and the house. He'd taken off his jacket and tie, and pushed up the sleeves of his khaki shirt. Annie glanced at his tanned forearms, at his strong yet graceful hands that so capably gripped the wheel. He looked comfortable in his faded jeans. Annie was wearing her navy slacks—mundane but perfectly serviceable. She'd clipped her hair back firmly with two barrettes, ready for the wind that buffeted the open Jeep. She was dressed in her usual sensible way, behaving in her usual prepared manner. But why couldn't she be more like Derrek? There was a sense of freedom about him now that Annie longed to share. Suddenly she reached up and yanked out her barrettes. Her hair whipped around her face, a strand somehow managing to work its way into her mouth. But she didn't feel free at all, just tangled and messy.

"I talked to Vance Forester today," Derrek said. "I called him up and raked him over the coals. If it were completely up to me, I'd fire him. I can't do that, but at least he'll keep his mouth shut from now on. I can guarantee you that much."

Annie pushed her bangs out of her eyes.

"I could have handled Vance myself," she answered.

"You don't have to do everything alone, Annie. There's nothing wrong with accepting a little help now and then." His tone was mild, but Annie flushed.

"I *am* grateful," she said awkwardly. She wanted to be open and easy with him, but she didn't know how. She hadn't had any practice. Lapsing into silence, she watched as this time Derrek followed the signs into Santa Fe. Earth-toned houses nestled among the piñon and juniper trees on the outskirts, but soon the Jeep was moving along busy streets. Derrek turned into a side street where there was less traffic and parked quickly and expertly. He came around to Annie's side while she was still fighting with the buckle on her seat belt.

"I know what you're going to tell me," he said. "You're going to say that you can climb in and out of my Jeep just fine by yourself."

Annie bit her lip in exasperation. That was exactly what she'd been about to say. She had her seat belt off now, and she felt at a complete impasse with Derrek. He stood on the curb close beside her, not giving her any room to maneuver herself out of the vehicle. She pulled at the strands of her hair, trying to rearrange them.

"I like you windblown," he said. He put his hands around her waist and swiveled her body toward him. His eyes were filled with laughter even though he maintained a solemn expression.

"Why are you so afraid of me, Annabel? Haven't I proven to you how harmless I am?"

There was nothing harmless about him. He had a firm hold on her and obviously didn't intend to relinquish it in a hurry.

"I'm just not good at this sort of thing," she mumbled.

He looked interested. "What sort of thing are we talking about?" One of his fingers probed experimentally along her side. She tried to think straight.

"It's pretty obvious what we're talking about," she declared. "All this male-female interaction and so forth."

"Hmm." His thumb had found the beginning of her rib cage. "You're not ticklish, are you?" he inquired. "So far you haven't even cracked a smile."

"I'm very ticklish under the proper circumstances," she said grumpily.

"When you're not worried about male-female interaction," he suggested.

"I haven't had the greatest of luck with personal relationships," she stated. "I think it's much better to keep things on a business level."

"Annie, don't make the mistake of comparing me with someone like Vance Forester. I'm not like that at all."

"I know you're not! That's the whole point. Vance I can handle. But you..." Annie squirmed under Derrek's hands. She had to stop blurting out all her feelings. He was laughing at her openly now.

"So you don't think you can handle me, Annie Brooke. But at least you should give it a try. Who knows, you might have fun." He swung her down from the Jeep. She was decidedly unsteady on her feet, but determined not to show it. Derrek began to lead her along a narrow winding street. Stately cottonwood trees offered their shade, and lilac blooms cascaded over a wall of crumbling adobe. A string of dried chili peppers hanging from one of the doorways made a splash of red.

They came to a beautiful plaza. It was a large grassy square with old-fashioned lampposts and a variety of trees. White wrought-iron benches were placed invitingly along the brick walkways. Derrek tucked Annie's hand into the crook of his elbow and escorted her on a turn around the plaza.

She wandered musingly beside him, enjoying the rich sense of the past all about her. The storefronts nearby preserved the old adobe style, and it was easy for her to imagine that she'd stepped into another time. Derrek painted in the details for her.

"Just think, Annie," he said, "this plaza was once the end of the Sante Fe Trail. The wagon trains would roll in here all the way from Independence, Missouri. Pretty soon everyone would be celebrating in the saloons and dance halls. Billy the Kid was chained up here once—did you know that?"

Annie nodded, then sighed. She was no longer thinking about the past. Coupled with the turbulence Derrek made her feel, New Mexico was *still* the Wild West. Unwillingly her gaze wandered over him as they walked. He certainly did look good in a snug faded pair of jeans. In profile his rough-hewn features were emphasized, but the lines of weariness in his face had eased. He turned his head and gave her a slow lingering smile. Before she could be seduced by his smile, she wrenched her eyes away and stared straight in front of her. She decided it was best just to watch where she was going.

They made another leisurely tour around the plaza. But when Derrek started on a third loop, Annie cleared her throat. "There isn't much point to this," she said. "We're just walking around in circles."

"We're promenading," he answered. "There's a difference."

"All right, we're promenading," she acquiesced. "But why?"

Derrek chuckled.

"Do you always need a reason for everything, Annie? We're indulging in an old Spanish custom. Promenading on the plaza was one of the few ways strictly brought-up girls could enjoy some romance in their lives. But it was only accomplished correctly when the girls strolled in one direction and the boys the opposite. When their paths crossed they could flirt a little with each other." Derrek stopped and regarded Annie quizzically. "Maybe you and I should do this the right way," he said in a serious tone. "We'll walk in opposite directions and check each other out when we meet up. Here, just turn around—"

"Oh, no." She tightened her grip on his arm and made sure that they both stepped forward in unison. "Mating rituals are interesting to study," she said crisply, "but they're rather obsolete now, don't you think?"

"Not at all," he replied. "We just have different rituals today. We still need them so that we men and women can get together."

"Maybe that's fine for some people," Annie said. "Getting together, and all." She tried to walk on with determination, but Derrek slowed the pace.

"Did Vance Forester hurt you so much?" he asked quietly. Annie stopped and dropped abruptly onto one of the iron benches. Derrek sat down beside her, stretching out his legs and leaning back. He seemed to be waiting for her to answer his question. The leaves on the trees rustled as if they, too, wanted to know what she had to say for herself.

Annie shrugged impatiently. "It's not only Vance," she said, glancing at Derrek. "I was never in love with him, if that's what you're wondering. But relationships in general . . . they're just not for me. I can't see any use for them, not for me, anyway." She made an effort to sound matter-of-fact. Derrek rested an arm along the back of the bench, his hand not quite touching her.

"Someone must have hurt you badly," he said in a low voice. "If it wasn't Vance, then someone else."

She was annoyed at his probing, and frowned at him. "I don't have any tragic love affairs in my past," she retorted. "Nothing melodramatic in the least. But frankly I've never seen a relationship that worked. My parents' marriage was a failure. And I hear husbands and wives complaining all the time, their dreams about each other destroyed over the years. I think it's better not to dream about that type of thing at all." She crossed her ankles and stared down at her navy pumps. She had cleaned them up and polished them until they were as immaculate as ever.

"Well, now," Derrek said thoughtfully, "you're either a cynic, Annie Brooke, or a hopeless romantic. I can't figure out which."

Her head came up at this remark. "I'm not a romantic at all," she said firmly. But Derrek appeared to be following his own train of thought. He clasped his hands behind his head, gazing up through the tree branches as he spoke.

"It's perfectly logical," he murmured. "A young girl is bruised by her parents' divorce, and that makes her sensitive to other unhappy relationships. Deep down all she wants is someone to love her, but she's afraid to dream about that. Dreaming means she might be terribly disappointed and hurt someday. She can't risk that, and so she stifles all the passion inside her. But the passion is still there."

Annie clenched her fingers around the edge of the bench seat. "You're not talking about me," she said angrily. "You're just making up a story that sounds good to you!"

"Are you denying the passion inside you?" he asked, his voice so soft it was like a touch on her skin.

"Yes—no—" Annie drew in her breath, trying to steady herself. "Everyone has physical needs," she managed in a cool clinical tone. "The human body is simply built that way."

"You know that's not what I'm talking about, Annie. I'm talking about real passion—from the heart." Derrek half turned on the bench to face her. She clasped her hands tightly in her lap to hide their trembling. She felt raw, as if Derrek had exposed a wound. But Annie drew upon her courage and did not flinch away from him.

"All right, Derrek. Do you want me to tell you the truth? Sometimes it hurts a lot, knowing I'm not like other women, knowing that something is missing inside me, this passion you talk about. I hear love songs, but the words have no meaning for me. It's like hearing a foreign language. But then I remember that I have another kind of passion—my work, and what it can give to people." Annie straightened her back proudly. "I don't need you poking around in my life, trying to figure out what's wrong with me. Maybe there's nothing wrong. Maybe I've figured out the best way for a person to be happy!"

Derrek's hand moved gently over her shoulder, then lifted to brush the tumbled hair away from her cheek. "I'm not saying there's anything wrong with you, Annie. But I won't accept what you're saying. I know you have a capacity for passion—the intense personal kind. I can feel it."

Annie sat very still as his hand moved like a whisper over her hair. Always she had longed for someone to recognize that she *did* have feelings, that she was a warm person underneath her reserve. But now, when at last it had happened, she wanted to deny it. Because Derrek wasn't just talking about warmth here. He was talking about fire, the kind that could so easily burn out of control and consume a person.

But Derrek wouldn't relent, and tried another angle of attack on her. "Annie, you tell me passion is like a foreign language to you. But people come to New Mexico, you know, and they learn to speak Spanish. Any language just takes time and a little effort."

The tenderness in his expression was more dangerous than anything else. Annie stiffened herself against it. "You're stretching this analogy way too far. I suppose I should sign up for a class somewhere," she said mockingly. "Lessons in Love, or some such nonsense."

Derrek refused to be baited. "Maybe you should, at that," he returned. "I think you'd catch on pretty quickly. Maybe you just need the right teacher."

She'd left herself wide open for *that* remark, and its implication that Derrek was the teacher she needed.

"What about you?" she demanded. "If you're so well-balanced, why aren't you married by now with a couple of kids? Explain that to me." She was pleased when he looked confounded. It took him a moment to answer.

"I've had a few long-term relationships," he said at last. "They weren't anything spectacular, though. I always expected something more from them, something that never happened."

Annie gazed at him. "You really are a romantic, aren't you?" she asked in surprise. "You want bells to start clanging in your head."

Derrek smiled a little. "That's one way of putting it. Most of all, I just want to make sure I don't treat a woman the way my father treated my mother. Maybe that's held me back, but I'll tell you something, Annie. I'm not afraid to risk a relationship, not if I think it's worth the risk. It's too bad you can't feel the same way." He looked straight at her, so intently that she couldn't turn away. He seemed to be issuing a challenge again. But what did he want from her? What could she possibly give to a man like him?

"What's going on over there?" she asked, changing the subject decisively. She pointed to a low adobe building across the street. It ran the length of an entire block and had an overhanging porch, supported by thick round wooden pillars, under which a few dozen native men and women had spread out their wares.

"That's the Palace of the Governors," Derrek told her. "It's been standing since 1610. Now it's a museum, and you'll probably want to investigate it."

"No," Annie said, surprising herself. "No museums today—nothing work-related. Just tell me about the people doing the selling there. They seem so remote somehow, as if they're only tolerating the tourists who come by. It must be tedious to sit there and do all that tolerating."

Derrek nodded reflectively. "They're Pueblo Indians, and they've had to endure a lot of harsh intrusion over the centuries. Anyway, they come here to sell their crafts. Let me show you how beautiful their jewelry is."

"Wait—" Annie protested, but Derrek had already grasped her hand and was pulling her across the brick-laid street. They dodged a car and ended up under the vast porch. Annie truly felt like an intruder. She was such a private person herself that she always respected other private people. Even though the Pueblo Indians had come here to sell their wares, Annie recognized in their faces the inward turning of spirit that she knew in herself. She did not want to intrude any further.

Derrek suffered no such qualms and dragged her along with him. This afternoon he had poked and prodded at Annie's emotions quite mercilessly. With the same ease and confidence he had used to dissect her, he now knelt before a display of silver and turquoise jewelry.

"Look, Annie, this is a squash-blossom necklace," he said. She leaned down beside him, examining the ornate necklace that was laden with turquoise stones.

Delicately worked points of silver all around it did, indeed, give the impression of squash blossoms. It was lovely. She leaned down for a closer look and teetered a little. Derrek straightened and put his arm around her waist. He held on even after she'd regained her balance, pointing out other pieces of jewelry spread out on a black cloth—heavy bracelets, whimsical brooches, one depicting a coyote howling at a golden moon, exquisite pierced earrings so small they could only be meant for a child.

"That's another custom you'll find in New Mexico," Derrek explained. "You'll see little girls and even babies with their ears pierced."

An elderly Pueblo woman was sitting in a low canvas chair beside the display. She was wearing a bright print dress, heavy turquoise bracelets and pink sneakers, and though her face was lined with fine wrinkles, only a few strands of gray ran through her black hair. She smiled at Derrek as she crocheted a small yellow blanket, perhaps a gift for a grandchild, Annie thought. Derrek grinned back at the woman, at the same time tightening his arm around Annie's waist. The woman's smile broadened, but she didn't miss a beat with her crochet hook.

Annie tried to pull away from Derrek without success. He just held on tighter.

"What do you want me to buy for you?" he asked.

"Nothing!" she exclaimed. The old woman's face wore a deadpan expression now, but she seemed to enjoy watching Derrek and Annie.

"I know you want a memento of our day together," Derrek went on seriously. "Go ahead, *querida*, choose something for yourself."

"I don't want anything," Annie said between gritted teeth. "You're a museum trustee, and I can't accept gifts from you. And what did you just call me?"

"Querida," he murmured, drawing her even closer to him. His voice sounded outrageously seductive.

"What does that mean?" Annie asked in exasperation, her face heating up again at his nearness.

"Well, it's a word in a foreign language," he said wickedly. "You'll have to take some lessons before you can understand it."

"You're the one who should learn a few things—about independent women," she retorted. She struggled to free herself, but Derrek merely grinned and held on to her more tenaciously, his hand like a clamp around her waist. He was infuriating. At the museum Annie was used to managing her staff with coolness and efficiency. One remark from her was enough to get results from even the most stubborn employee. But Derrek wasn't someone she could manage at all. The Indian woman went on with her crocheting as if it were the most important thing in the world, yet her mouth twitched with suppressed amusement.

"We can't leave until you choose something, Annie," Derrek insisted. "How about that beaded necklace?"

The Indian woman set down her crocheting and shook her head at his selection. "No, that is not the right choice," she said gravely. "I will show you something else, if you wish."

"We'd be very interested," Derrek answered. "I want this to be the perfect gift."

Annie tried giving Derrek a jab with her elbow, but he was holding on to her too firmly and she couldn't get any leverage. The woman reached down among the necklaces and picked one out. She handed it to Derrek in silence.

"Ah, yes," he murmured, resting it in his palm with the silver chain dangling over his fingers. "I believe this is just right."

Annie looked at the necklace. It was very simple: a single silver chain and a small turquoise pendant roughly molded in the shape of a heart. But its very simplicity made it special, and the stone was a deep, rich blue green.

Derrek looked at Annie.

"Do you like it?" he asked.

"Yes, of course, it's lovely. But Derrek..." she protested as he reached around and fastened the chain's clasp behind her neck. His fingers brushed against her skin and then he stepped back to observe her, taking his time.

"Yes, it's the gift I want," he said at last. He turned toward the woman again. "It suits her perfectly, don't you think?"

The old woman nodded.

"I knew it would suit her," she said complacently, holding up a tarnished mirror. Annie gazed at her reflection, and her hand closed around the turquoise stone. She had a perverse impulse to yank it off. But she found it difficult to resist the simple beauty of the necklace. She traced the shape of the heart, wishing it didn't feel so natural resting against her skin.

Derrek and the woman began conducting a financial transaction with obvious enjoyment on both sides. Annie opened her mouth to stop the proceeding, but the woman was speaking again, and her words stunned Annie.

"You have made a wise gift, a heart to represent the love between you. I can see the love, and it is very strong."

CHAPTER SIX

BOTH ANNIE AND DERREK were effectively silenced by the pronouncement. Only the woman herself was unconcerned. She picked up her crocheting again and retreated into her own private world. She seemed completely unaware of the havoc she had just wreaked in Annie. Or perhaps she *was* aware of it, for a rather satisfied smile played around her mouth.

Annie turned and walked blindly away. She stepped out from under the porch and into the mellow evening light. She made it across the street and back to the plaza before Derrek caught up with her.

"Hold on, Annie—"

"You had no right to do that, Derrek! I can't accept a gift from you."

He strolled beside her, thumbs hooked easily in the pockets of his jeans. "I don't think we're bending the rules that much," he remarked cheerfully. "And we're not bending them at all, if you consider what the woman said—that we're in love." There was a glint of humor in his eyes.

Annie brought herself up short and glared at him. "Don't make a joke out of it," she said furiously. "It's already been humiliating enough. How could she say something like that?"

"Well, now, maybe she sees possibilities you and I haven't thought about yet—possibilities we should explore."

Annie started walking again very rapidly. The turquoise heart bobbed up and down on her chest in rhythm with her agitation.

"You can laugh about it all you want," she said. "People don't fall in love after such a short time."

"Anything's possible," Derrek murmured as he kept pace with her. She could still hear the humor in his voice. Dammit, why couldn't she be flippant about this and just dismiss the whole thing with a genuine laugh of her own?

She couldn't, that was all. It wasn't in her nature. She had to explain things neatly and tidily, leaving no loose ends. Annie sighed.

"Derrek, I think it's time we drew the boundaries here. I can't flirt with you. I don't know how. I can't joke about things like love, and I certainly can't accept this necklace from you." She reached up and fumbled with the clasp at the back of her neck.

"No, Annie, please don't," Derrek said, his voice serious now. He took her elbow and steered her on down the walk. "That necklace was meant for you, only for you. It's a gift of friendship—how's that? But I wasn't joking entirely. We both know something is happening between us."

Annie didn't really want to continue this discussion. But she had to see it through to the end, to ensure there were no misunderstandings.

"Let's be realistic, Derrek," she said firmly. "Rational people can't describe their emotions as love after knowing each other less than two days." She glanced at her watch. "If you want to be exact, we've known each other precisely thirty-three hours and...and fourteen minutes. That's hardly enough time to reach any conclusions—"

"I was just about to say the same thing myself," Derrek interrupted her, leading her across another street. "We can't draw any conclusions about our feelings yet, one way or the other. After all, it's only been thirty-three hours and...sixteen minutes, on the nose."

"You're making fun of me again," Annie complained.

"I'm trying to make you see reason," Derrek said. "Authentic reason, not the rigid distorted brand of logic you're bound to come up with." He smiled at her companionably. Then he propelled her under another long porch and ushered her into a small dim Mexican restaurant.

"I'm not hungry," she began to protest, but nonetheless found herself sliding into a cramped booth across from him. She ignored the menu on the table in front of her and gazed expectantly at Derrek, waiting for him to go on. He took up a plastic container of honey, turning it thoughtfully in his hands.

"Well?" Annie demanded at last. "You might as well finish whatever you want to say to me. I'd really like to get this matter cleared up so we can go on to something else."

Derrek set down the honey and regarded her across the table. "All right, I'll tell you how I feel. I'm very attracted to you. I'm willing to admit that something might be happening between us, something that could grow. It's not a minor detail that we can just 'clear up.'"

Annie sat back, feeling exhausted and far too vulnerable. She stared down at the cheery red lettering on her menu. A waiter appeared, a stout middle-aged man with fleshy jowls and a thick bushy mustache. He looked like a benevolent sandy-haired walrus as he peered first at Annie and then at Derrek.

"Hello, Burt," Derrek said. "How's the green chili sauce today?"

"Spicy," Burt answered. "Almost as hot as the red chili." He rested his hands on his paunch and peered at Annie again. "I take it we're dealing with a novice here."

"Afraid so. Annie, this gentleman is Burt Campbell, and he's going to bring you a tall glass of milk. Just hang on to it, and you'll be fine tonight."

Annie didn't understand what Derrek was talking about, but felt as if she were about to undergo some bizarre initiation rite.

"I'm pleased to meet you, Burt," she said briskly. "If you don't mind, I'll skip the milk and whatever this sauce is you're talking about. I'll just have a cup of coffee and a grilled cheese sandwich."

Both men stared at her.

"I think the cook would be offended if I gave him an order like that," Burt said doubtfully.

"How about a tuna sandwich?" Annie queried without much hope.

Burt looked extremely doubtful now, and Derrek took charge. "I think Annie should have a plate of cheese enchiladas, with the green chili sauce on the side. And I'll have the chili *rellenos* and a beer."

Burt seemed relieved as he went off. Annie faced Derrek again. "I'm used to making my own decisions," she informed him with spirit. "And as far as something happening between us, Derrek...there's no chance of that."

He propped his elbows on the table. "You can't tolerate uncertainty, can you?" he asked. "Not knowing what's going to happen tomorrow, or the day after that. But it's all part of the excitement of life. Why not take a chance?"

He looked so devilishly attractive sitting across from her, and he also looked like the kind of person who took chances every day of his life. Annie herself relied on plans and schedules and agendas. She badly needed one of those right now. But with Derrek she felt as if she were about to go plunging off the edge of a cliff. How could she come up with an agenda for something like that?

"I don't want to be hurt," she blurted. "And if I don't know what's going to happen, I can't be prepared! I always have to prepare. Don't you see?"

He reached over and took one of her hands in his. "Annie, haven't you considered the fact that I might get hurt, too?"

That thought was simply incomprehensible to her. "It wouldn't happen," she stated flatly. "I'm just not the kind of woman that men break their hearts over." She tilted her chin. "And that's just fine with me. I don't want to break any hearts."

"Annie, you shouldn't undervalue yourself. You're worth loving, can't you see that?"

He had asked the one question she didn't know how to answer. Quickly she pulled her hand away from his.

"We're forgetting the real issue," she declared. "We're talking about our relationship here, and we're going to resolve it once and for all. I can think of five good reasons why everything should remain on a strictly business level between us. Number one—"

"Wait, let me do this," Derrek said. "Reason number one, I'm a museum trustee. Number two, you're a museum employee. Now, so far you don't have much of an argument. It's the next three reasons that are the real obstacles. You're afraid of life, you're afraid of me, and most of all, you're afraid of yourself. I think that just about covers everything, Annie." He sat back against the cracked vinyl of the booth and watched her. His words cut too deeply. It wasn't fair! Before Derrek she'd been going along through life quite well by herself. Oh, she'd always had plenty of self-doubts, but with her dedication to her work she'd been able to keep most of them at bay. She'd never truly had to face them before. Then yesterday she'd met Derrek, and from the first moment he had seemed determined to rip away all her defenses.

Annie closed her eyes briefly. When she opened them again, she was able to gaze steadily at Derrek.

"It doesn't matter what you say to me," she told him in a calm voice. "I'm not going to get involved with you."

He didn't argue this time. He only smiled at her with a piercing mixture of tenderness and humor, which was even harder to fight than words. But Annie had stated her position and she intended to stick by it.

Burt returned to the table bearing steaming platters of food. Annie's enchiladas looked delicious, the rolled tortillas buried under melted cheese, chunks of tomato and crisp shreds of lettuce. She decided she was hungry, after all, and took a good bite. The enchiladas were as delicious as they looked. As she chewed, she gazed speculatively at the dish of chili sauce Burt had given her. Feeling reckless, she dipped her next forkful liberally into the sauce and popped it into her mouth.

Instantly her throat was on fire. Her finger groped uselessly over the table until Burt arrived to rescue her with a glass of milk. She gulped down most of it.

Annie set down the glass, her eyes streaming. Burt's mustache was so bushy she couldn't see his mouth, but she could tell he was giving her an encouraging smile.

"I'll bring you a refill on that milk," he said. "It really does the trick, doesn't it?"

Annie nodded weakly. She picked up her fork again, but stayed well away from the chili sauce as she went on eating. She regarded Derrek in wonder as he ate his own spicy meal without even flinching—green chilis stuffed with cheese and fried in a crusty batter. Annie decided he must have a cast-iron interior.

The best part of the meal was a basket of sopapillas, which Burt placed on the table between them. The sopapillas were fluffy hollow pockets of dough, rather like popovers.

"Here, let me show you how this is done," Derrek said. He took a sopapilla, broke it open at one end and trickled honey inside it. Then he handed it to Annie.

She ate it with thorough enjoyment, the honey dripping over her fingers. She tried licking them surreptitiously, only to find Derrek watching her again, a look of amusement on his face. Annie wiped her fingers on a paper napkin in the proper way, and yet that wasn't nearly as satisfying. She broke open another sopapilla, squeezed in a generous amount of honey, and this time licked her fingers with total disregard for Derrek's entertainment.

When they left the restaurant Annie waved goodbye to Burt. Night had fallen as they lingered over dinner, and the air was cool and fresh. Lights glimmered around the plaza, and the lazy sound of someone's laughter drifted on the spring breeze. Derrek clasped Annie's hand and led her back along the winding streets.

She felt disoriented in the darkness, even though light splashed out from doorways. Along the wall of one building the window shutters had been flung open wide, and inside was a restaurant where people were sitting at wooden tables eating and talking. Mingled with the laughter and chatter were the sounds of plates and silverware clinking. The windows reached low to the ground, as if inviting passersby to step inside and join the fun. But Annie and Derrek remained outside in the shadows, watching the scene through the windows as if they were in a darkened theater and a play was unfolding on the stage before them. Everyone looked so happy and carefree, except for one woman sitting at a crowded table. She stared with weary concentration into her glass, as if wishing herself far away from her noisy companions. Annie felt uncomfortable, like an eavesdropper, and she pulled Derrek along the street with her.

"There are so many people in the world," she said quietly. "Each one has joy and sadness the rest of us can only guess at. How can we ever really know what another person is going through?''

''We can come right out and ask,'' Derrek said.

His practical suggestion punctured her reflective mood. She was annoyed. ''You can't just do that,'' she protested. ''You can't just go and barrel into people's lives!''

''Why not?'' he asked reasonably. ''Most of the time that's exactly what people need.''

Annie moved her fingers restlessly in Derrek's hand. That was what he'd done to her—he had barreled into her life, sweeping aside the barriers she had erected so carefully. But that wasn't what she needed. It wasn't what she needed at all!

''Where's the Jeep?'' she asked, glancing about as they turned down a deserted street. ''We should have reached it by now.''

''We're walking in the opposite direction from it,'' Derrek told her. ''It's early yet, Annie, and I thought you and I could do some meandering. Only now I suppose you'll tell me that you don't believe in meandering.''

''As a matter of fact, I don't...'' Annie's voice trailed off as Derrek leaned her against an adobe wall, still warm from the sun. His finger traced a path along her cheek, sending a delicious ripple of sensation through her. But in a defensive reflex she twisted her head away. ''I told you—I don't want to get involved with you,'' she said shakily.

''Annie, we're already involved in something together. Why don't we find out what it is?'' He bent his head over hers in the starlight, his lips touching her eyebrow.

She pressed back against the nubby surface of the wall. "Please, Derrek," she whispered, "let's stop now. I'm no good at this."

"I can show you what to do, Annie, but I think you'll find that it comes naturally to you." His voice was low and husky as he gazed down at her. He took both of her hands in his, raising them until they rested on his shoulders. Hesitantly Annie slid her arms higher until her hands were clasped behind his neck. It was like a dance without music, Derrek's steps unfamiliar but enticing her to follow. Warnings clamored inside Annie, telling her to resist his lead. But his arms gathered her close. For a moment she hid herself against him, her heart beating thickly in her chest. Then, slowly, she raised her face.

Derrek's mouth brushed over hers, teasing with its gentleness. Annie's eyelids drifted downward and she was alive only to Derrek's touch, his nearness, his heady masculine scent. When his lips moved away from her, she arched her head back in silent appeal for more.

Now he kissed her throat, his breath warm on her skin. A deep hard coldness seemed to be dissolving inside her, painfully and reluctantly. In dismay Annie felt tears stinging behind her eyelids and she tensed herself against them. But Derrek's mouth descended on hers again and the pain inside her began to melt away along with the coldness. She didn't move, almost didn't breathe, as if Derrek's touch were too fragile a thing. He lifted his hand and with a finger blotted away the tear that had escaped unheeded down her cheek.

"Kiss me back, Annie," he murmured, and her body stiffened all over again.

"Derrek . . . I can't . . ."

"Trust me. Trust yourself." His voice was soft. She felt so awkward and unsure, but he didn't rush her. Experimentally she moved her lips against his, learning the firm shape of them. And after that everything was as natural as he'd promised. Need flared up inside her. She tangled her hands in Derrek's hair, bringing his head down closer to hers. She tasted the clean warmth of his mouth, thrilling at his groan of pleasure. The need and longing inside her fanned up, demanding more fulfillment even as Derrek's lips bruised hers. Oh, yes, he had been right—there was passion inside her.

But it was much too powerful and overwhelming. All her long-held instincts of fear struggled to the surface, and with a gasp she wrenched away from Derrek. She turned and pressed her face and one hand against the rough wall, trembling as if she would break. Hot tears scalded her face, coming silently, without sobs. She had not cried since she was a very young child, and she didn't know why she was crying now. Inside her the coldness was back, lodged stubbornly in its familiar place. But from somewhere nearby came the pungent scent of lilacs, and Derrek was smoothing the damp wisps of hair away from her cheek.

"I have something I want to show you, Annie, a few blocks from here. It's a building I designed, and it's being constructed now. I'd like you to see it."

She listened to his voice, intensely grateful for the note it struck—casual and conversational, as if they hadn't been locked in one another's arms only a moment ago. She needed that now, after their shattering kiss. Furtively she wiped her cheeks with a tissue. Derrek stepped back, waiting for her on the sidewalk. No more tears came, as if she had possessed only a limited supply of them. Her eyes felt too dry now. Taking a deep, quavering breath, she joined Derrek and together they walked down the street.

He didn't speak, and he didn't clasp her hand in the relaxed way he had before. He didn't touch her at all, as if aware of her need to walk separately from him. No longer was he pushing her or trying to expose her emotions. Perhaps he realized that he'd already pushed her too far.

They came to the building, and Annie saw row after row of wooden beams rising in the moonlight like the blanched bones of a skeleton. The effect was stark and yet beautiful. Annie walked toward the construction site, maneuvering around a stack of boards. Derrek took her arm, but it was only to guide her over the uneven ground. Once they'd stepped onto the concrete foundation of the building, he moved away from her again. The distance between them was beginning to feel strained.

Annie cleared her throat. "What kind of building is this going to be?" she asked.

"It's an office for a law firm," he told her. "Over here—this will be the reception area. Do you see how much light will be coming in through the windows? Nothing is worse than working in an office that doesn't have enough light."

Annie tried to picture how the windows would be, and yet all she saw was more wooden studs. This place was Derrek's vision, not hers, but she could enjoy the enthusiasm in his voice. He led her through the building, pointing out the myriad details that had taken shape in his mind. Soon they would be realities in plaster and wood and glass.

"Up there, Annie—no, look higher and more toward your right—that's where the solar collection panels will be. Can you think of a better way to heat a building than using the sun's energy?"

She craned her neck, staring at the rafters that jutted above her and trying very hard to see what Derrek saw.

"Solar energy is tremendously exciting, Annie," he went on. "Someday you'll see incredible things. Solar-powered automobiles—just think about that!"

Annie listened to him, hearing something familiar in his tone. It was passion—the kind she herself understood. Passion for work, passion for dreams. She had thought Derrek was so easygoing, but he possessed intensity, too. She watched as he grasped one of the beams, testing it for strength. His tall lean frame was silhouetted in a shaft of moonlight. Annie felt drawn to him, but still there was a tension between them.

"You're working on something else right now, aren't you?" she asked. "A design for a house? I saw it today on your drafting board."

"You're right. I'm in the middle of designing a home for a family in Albuquerque."

Annie looked at the solid beams all about her. "I think you've chosen a wonderful thing to do with your life," she said.

Derrek began to pace restlessly. "It's what I've always wanted to do," he told her. "But I'm already behind schedule on those house plans. The Richards foundation is demanding more and more of my time. The chaos there seems to be growing, not diminishing. My father couldn't have planned his revenge any better."

Annie recoiled from the harsh words. "Surely he didn't want any kind of revenge on you, Derrek! You're his son."

He didn't speak for a long moment, his head bent down. Then he answered her. "My father didn't think of me as a son. He saw me as a competitor. I never wanted to be an artist, but he still felt threatened by me. Maybe he was afraid I'd demand too much attention from my mother, or that I'd develop a talent he didn't have."

Annie thought about her own father. On each of her birthdays he'd sent her a card, but she could no longer remember what he looked like. He had made it clear from the beginning that he didn't want Annie to visit him and his second wife.

"Derrek, at least you had a father who was around," she said earnestly. "Good or bad, at least you knew him. He never abandoned you!"

Derrek raised his head and gazed at her. His face was cast in shadows. "You don't know what you're talking about, Annie. You don't know at all." There was a bleakness in his voice. Annie stared back at him, not understanding his pain and yet wishing she could take it away from him. She wanted to hear his rich easy laughter again, and his excitement about capturing energy from the sun.

"I think it would be better if you talked about what's bothering you," she said in a low voice. "You tell me that I don't understand. Maybe I *would* understand if you explained it some more."

Derrek shook his head. "You really think it's simple, don't you? I suppose this is another one of your projects. Let's see...Annabel Brooke's Five-Step Plan to Resolve the Richards' Family Crisis."

Annie took a sharp breath, stung by his sarcasm. "I didn't mean anything like that," she returned. "You're the one who says people should barrel into other people's lives. That's what I'm doing—barreling. I'm just not very good at it yet."

"Every rule has its exceptions," he said curtly. "This is one case where you shouldn't intrude."

Annie felt hurt and angry. He had encouraged her to reach out, and now he was rejecting her. But she could be stubborn.

"The bitterness inside you is eating you up, Derrek. You have to get it out somehow," she insisted.

"I've already told you too much about Carlisle Richards as it is. I'm going to stop before it's too late."

She crossed over to him. "Too late for what, Derrek?" she asked softly. "What kind of secret are you trying to hide?" She lifted a hand to touch him, but he drew away from her.

"It's going to remain a secret," he said, his voice rough. "Stop treating this like a problem you can solve, Annie. It's not like that." He stared down at her, his eyes glittering in the moonlight. His gaze held no gentleness for her, not anymore. She clenched her hands, feeling powerless. If only she could break through to him! They stood together and yet apart in the darkness of night, so many tensions vibrating between them—Annie's fears, and Derrek's bitterness and frustration. She didn't know how to overcome all that. Without speaking, she and Derrek walked back to the Jeep. Still in silence they drove toward the house he detested so much. The magic of Santa Fe was left far behind them.

CHAPTER SEVEN

ANNIE POKED HER HEAD out the door of her bedroom. She listened for a moment, but the only sound she heard was a bird chattering from the patio. Next she strode down the hallway, narrowing her eyes against the dazzling sunlight that poured through the windows. Usually Annie was a morning person, but not today. She didn't want to contend with anything or anyone—certainly not Derrek. But when she pushed open the door of the kitchen, she saw him seated at the table with papers and file folders strewn all about him. His hair was rumpled, his eyes shadowed with tiredness.

They looked at each other. After their return from Santa Fe last evening, they'd bidden one another good night in stiff politeness. This morning the atmosphere between them was still charged, like air weighted with electricity before the breaking of a storm.

Annie came into the room and made a clatter as she poured herself a cup of coffee.

"Can you hold the noise down? I'm trying to work in here," Derrek said irritably, thumbing through a ragged file folder.

Annie continued to stand at the counter, sipping the hot liquid. Derrek hauled a briefcase onto the table and started poking through it. He muttered under his breath, and Annie caught snatches of "blasted foundation...budget projections..." Then, "What the devil is this?" His voice had jumped several decibels. Frowning, he was holding a familiar blue folder and leafing through its contents. Annie set down her cup.

"That's my report to the board of trustees," she said proudly. "The one about the feasibility of a museum park, incorporating that vacant lot and the old wool mill. I'm surprised you haven't read it yet, Derrek."

Looking disgruntled, he started reading it now. Annie went to the table and pulled out a chair to sit across from him. She clasped her hands in front of her, watching Derrek, waiting with pleasurable anticipation for his response. She'd spent weeks preparing her proposal, and with great hope had mailed off a copy to each one of the trustees. Derrek's reaction, however, was to groan and slap the folder down on the table.

"Thirty pages, single spaced and crammed with small type," he complained. "You'd need a magnifying glass to get through this thing."

Annie retrieved her report. "I used small print on purpose," she declared. "I had a great deal of important information to present, and I wanted to keep the pages down to a reasonable number. And, look—did you see this chart on page sixteen? I used a spread sheet, and I've projected capitalization costs over a three-year period." She gazed in contentment at the profusion of grid lines, the many columns of data and the detailed figures calculated to the last penny.

"Annie, I'll have to be blunt with you," Derrek said. "What you've put together here is the worst presentation I've ever seen. It's far too technical. It's also ponderous and incredibly confusing. In short, no human being should be subjected to the punishment of wading through it—no matter what crime he or she has committed.''

Annie clutched the report protectively. She started to protest, but Derrek kept on talking. ''Here, take a look at this,'' he said, pushing a sheet of bright yellow paper toward her. ''This is Vance Forester's proposal to the trustees. Tell me what you think of it.''

Annie stared down at the sheet of paper. At the top was a sketch of an impressive-looking building with wings projecting from either side; below the sketch were large bold letters that proclaimed ''The ALL NEW Caroline Darcy Museum.'' Short choppy sentences down the rest of the page announced that a brand-new building for the museum was the direction of the future—''Increased revenues, prestige, power in the art world. The time to move is NOW!''

Annie glanced up. ''This is like a cheap advertisement,'' she said indignantly. ''Surely none of the trustees would take this seriously!'' She pushed the paper away with a contemptuous motion.

''It's eye-catching,'' Derrek said. ''It gets Vance's point across in thirty seconds instead of thirty pages. Don't you see, Annie? When your report arrived in the mail, I took one look at it and buried it in my briefcase. I forgot all about it, probably on purpose. But when this flier came in, one glance was all I needed to get its message. And that message has stayed with me, at the back of my mind.''

She couldn't believe what she was hearing. "My report has substance," she declared. "All you have to do is *read* it—"

"That's the problem, right there," Derrek interrupted brusquely. "Your ideas might be worthy, but no one's going to read them presented like that. You show absolutely no mercy for your audience—no sense of connection at all between yourself and the reader. Brevity, Annie. Brevity."

Annie clutched her report tightly. Then she placed it on the table, smoothing out the dents she'd made in the blue folder. It was a dark sober blue, as befitted the seriousness of the pages inside.

Derrek stood up, stretching his arms and rubbing his neck. He went to refill his coffee cup, then leaned against the counter. In spite of his relaxed stance, his muscles seemed taut. The lines of his face were hard and unyielding in the morning light.

"You know, Annie," he said, "this report of yours represents the larger problem you have. You're very restrained around people. You don't even try to make a connection."

Annie scraped back her chair and stood to face him. "I respect other people and their privacy," she defended herself.

"Listen, Annie. You want to be director of the museum. To do the job right you'd have to be a diplomat, a politician and a public-relations expert all rolled into one. That includes perpetually convincing all sorts of people to contribute funds to your cause. You'd have to know how to be charming and persuasive at the same time. I'm not sure you have what it takes."

She gripped the back of her chair. She had always trusted in one thing—her ability to do a good job at the museum. Derrek was questioning that, and undermining all her dreams.

"I can learn," she asserted. "I can learn whatever I need to know."

"This isn't something you can turn into one of your projects," he said implacably. "Either it comes naturally to you or it doesn't."

Annie shoved her chair against the table, then marched over to the counter. She tilted her head defiantly at Derrek.

"You can't change the rules just to suit yourself," she said, her voice shaking with anger. "Yesterday you told me that expressing passion was like mastering another language. If I can learn that, surely I can learn how to deal with others!"

Derrek gazed down at her, his eyes on her mouth. Now the lines of his face seemed to soften a little.

"Well, Annie," he murmured, "last night you did show me your passion. I can't argue with you there."

Color stained her cheeks. She pressed her lips together as if that would somehow obliterate the lush fullness of her mouth. When she spoke again it was in a stiff tone.

"I'm just asking you not to make assumptions about me. Give me a chance to prove myself."

Derrek propped both arms on the counter. "All right," he said carelessly, surprising her. "Tonight I have to go to a fund-raiser for the Richards Foundation. You can come with me and show me what you know how to do."

"Tonight?" she echoed in disbelief. "But that's too soon. I couldn't possibly be ready in time—"

"As a museum director, you'd constantly have to do things like this on the spur of the moment," he pointed out. She stared at the Spanish tiles that formed an intricate pattern of curling vines and flowers around the edge of the counter. Annie was good at handling painstaking details behind the scenes, but she'd always avoided the spotlight. Derrek was issuing her a challenge, one he thought she couldn't meet. She would prove him wrong!

"Very well," she said with determination. "What sort of fund-raiser is this? Are we talking about a dinner? Perhaps some kind of dancing afterward?"

Derrek shrugged. "I don't know. We'll just see what happens when we get there."

"But what do you expect from me tonight? I need specifics."

He considered this for a moment. "I expect you to act like a museum director," Derrek said. He wasn't being very helpful.

"I didn't bring an evening dress. I'll need to do some shopping in Santa Fe," she told him.

"No problem. I plan on making a trip there around one o'clock. You can ride in with me." Derrek stretched again and crossed to sit at the table. He pulled several file folders toward him, frowning down at them and effectively dismissing her presence. But the gauntlet had been thrown, and Annie had accepted the challenge to prove herself.

She wheeled around and strode out of the kitchen. She reached her workroom, shutting the door behind her and slamming the lock into place. Automatically she took up her jeweler's loupe and her scalpel, bending over the painting. The turquoise heart around her neck swung forward, surprising her into almost dropping the scalpel. She tightened her fingers just in time to avoid making a slash in the canvas.

Annie swore softly, backing away before she could do any real damage. She couldn't explain to herself why she'd worn the necklace all night, even as she slept. Now she unfastened the clasp with impatient fingers and pushed the turquoise heart deep into her pocket.

But she was still too rattled to work. She went to the deep-set window and kneeled on the frayed cushion along the ledge. She pressed her forehead against the warm pane and closed her eyes. Her stomach churned with apprehension about tonight. She'd never been good at dealing with people; her strength lay in self-reliance. But now she needed new skills, skills that would prove to Derrek she should be director of the museum.

The blood pumped inside her.

"Dammit, I'm going to succeed!" Annie exclaimed out loud. She pushed herself away from the window. This time when she picked up her scalpel, her hands were steady. She bent over the painting and lost herself in work.

ANNIE WAS WAITING outside the house at exactly one o'clock. She had used her travel iron to press her navy skirt and jacket, needing to feel businesslike and professional as she set out on her shopping expedition. She climbed into the Jeep and glanced at her watch, but it was several moments before Derrek strolled out of the house. He wore a tie, knotted crookedly at the collar of his shirt. His cowboy boots crunched over the gravel of the drive and he swung into the Jeep. He deposited a small paper sack in her lap.

"What's this?" she asked suspiciously.

"You didn't have any breakfast," he remarked, "and you didn't come out for lunch. You'll have to eat something sooner or later."

She opened the sack and examined the contents. A thick sandwich, a small box of raisins and a dill pickle wrapped in a piece of crinkled foil. Annie munched on the pickle as Derrek started the Jeep and headed down the road.

"Thank you," she said politely.

"You're welcome," he answered with equal politeness, turning onto the highway and picking up speed. Annie unwrapped the sandwich. The bread was the heavy, sprouted-grain type she'd seen in the refrigerator, and slathered liberally with peanut butter and strawberry preserve. It was very different from the sort of sandwich Annie made for herself. She usually spread her fillings so thinly over the bread that she could hardly tell what they were. Now she bit into Derrek's generous sandwich and realized she'd never known how good peanut butter could taste.

She glanced over at him, but he seemed lost in his own thoughts. She moved restlessly in her seat, wanting to tear down the barrier he had erected. How could

Derrek complain about *her* reticence? He was much better at shutting people out than she was.

Annie was left to her peanut-butter-and-jelly sandwich, which she'd polished off by the time they reached Santa Fe. When Derrek stopped near the plaza, she tucked the box of raisins inside her purse and scrambled down from the Jeep.

"I'll pick you up here at five-thirty," he said, then hesitated. He seemed about to say something else, but in the end he merely gave her a faint smile and the Jeep roared off again.

Annie stood on the sidewalk, smoothing herself out after the jolting ride. Then she combed her hair, straightened her shoulders and set off at her usual pace, brisk and efficient. It was easy to find the kind of place where she liked to shop. She gravitated naturally to an unprepossessing store tucked away by itself on a side street. Annie crossed through the doorway, finding much what she'd expected—clothes in subdued colors and practical materials that wouldn't wrinkle or bunch up. As she lingered by the dress racks, a salesclerk approached.

"May I assist you?" the woman asked pleasantly. Everything about her appearance was faultless and subdued. She could have been anywhere between the age of thirty-five and fifty, her skin soft and plump like freshly risen dough. Her brown hair was set in attractive but rigid curls, and her dark green polyester pantsuit looked fresh from the dry cleaner's. She was the kind of salesclerk who usually inspired confidence in Annie. But today something was wrong; Annie was annoyed rather than reassured by the woman's blandness.

"Well," Annie began, "I'm looking for something formal and elegant."

The woman sent a practiced eye over her and didn't waste any time. "I have just the thing for you," she said, moving systematically down the racks. "Here we are—this should be your size." She held up a simple tasteful dress in black rayon velvet. Annie nodded. This was exactly what she might have picked out for herself. She took it into the dressing room.

A few moments later she emerged and turned slowly in front of the mirror. The dress was impeccable. It had a high neckline and long narrow sleeves, with a gently billowing skirt. Annie looked neat and well-groomed. The black color washed out her complexion a bit, but that was nothing unusual for her. All the colors in Annie's wardrobe had the same dulling effect.

"It's perfect," the saleswoman decided. "Exactly the right style for you—discreet understated quality."

Annie stared into the mirror for another moment. Yes, she certainly looked discreet. The dress would be a safe choice, a wise investment. It would not embarrass her tonight, or make her stand out in any way. But suddenly that wasn't how Annie wanted to look. For once in her life she *wanted* to stand out!

It was an exhilarating feeling. Annie marched back to the dressing room. She replaced the gown on its hanger, and when she emerged she addressed the saleswoman firmly.

"This isn't what I had in mind. I'll just keep looking, thank you." She departed the store with a sense of relief and walked briskly down the street. The air was so warm that she took off her jacket and tucked it over her arm. Hopefully she examined all the shop windows she came upon. She saw cotton dresses in sunny pastels, other dresses in hand-loomed weaves, safari skirts and blouses that looked ready for adventure. But she didn't see anything she could possibly wear tonight.

This wasn't going to be an easy task. She had to find something special, a dress that would change her image. Reaching into her purse, she took out her raisins and ate them distractedly as she walked. The raisins were satisfying but didn't inspire her with any brilliant ideas.

She went onward, surrounded by beauty. The sky was a brilliant eggshell blue; the adobe walls took the gold of the sun and mellowed it, absorbing it into their own tawny brown and terra-cotta. Everywhere Annie looked she saw color. The chili peppers hanging from overhead beams were a glossy red, while porch pillars and window frames sported coats of bright turquoise paint. Walking in the shade under a long porch, she saw jewel tones of silken cloth flashing in a window— ruby, amethyst, sapphire, all the hues Annie loved but had never worn. She looked at the stylized mannequins flaunting those vivid silk dresses, then glanced up at the sign over the door of the shop: Carlotta's, spelled out in an exuberant script. Annie pushed open the door.

Inside, the racks of skirts, blouses and dresses shimmered with more color. Annie didn't see anyone in the shop, so she was startled when a disembodied female voice floated to her.

"Be with you in a minute! Just make yourself at home. I'm having a sale on madras shorts, by the way. Two pairs for the price of one."

Annie glanced at the colorful shorts stacked on a table. It occurred to her that she didn't even own a pair of shorts. Then she heard a rustle from one of the racks, and watched as a statuesque blonde came into view.

"Had to tack up a hem," the woman explained, gathering back her long tumble of curls. "Can you imagine what it's like to have a customer try on a skirt and half the hem is hanging down?"

Annie shook her head, taking stock of the other woman. Her wild yellow hair didn't look like a shade that would occur naturally on any human being, but somehow that made it all the more appealing. She was wearing a slinky knit dress in wine red that hugged every one of her impressive curves. Everything about her was extravagant, from her impossibly long finger-nails to her stiletto heels. She had a broad face, and her broad smile made up for any conventional lack of beauty.

"I'm Carlotta," she said. "Well, it's Charlotte, ac-tually, but don't you think Carlotta is better for a fancy-dress shop? Those shorts are really a bargain. We're going to have a hot summer."

Annie gripped her purse with determination and gazed steadily at Charlotte. "My name is Annie, and

I need something more complicated than a pair of shorts," she said. "I'd like to change my image a little. No, make that a lot. I want to be more...exciting. Do you think you could help me? I only have a few hours to get the job done." Annie listened to herself, rather overwhelmed because she hadn't intended to make such a sweeping request.

Charlotte looked intrigued. "You want clothes, hair—the works?" she asked.

"Yes, the works," Annie agreed, although she wasn't sure exactly what that entailed. "You see, I'm going to a fund-raiser tonight—with a man. Basically...I'd like to impress him." Annie clamped her mouth shut before she could reveal anything more. There was something about Charlotte's expansive friendly manner that encouraged confidences. Now Charlotte circled slowly around Annie, looking her up and down with a speculative expression.

"We can do a lot with you," she said, a gleam in her hazel eyes. "In fact, we can knock this man of yours right off his feet."

"He's not exactly my man," Annie clarified, but Charlotte waved this explanation aside.

"Honey, after he sees what you're going to look like tonight, he *will* be." She turned to a slim redhead who had just rushed through the door. "Beverly," she called, "will you run across the street and get me a couple of things? Here's a list." Charlotte scribbled on a scrap of paper and handed it to her assistant. "I'm going to have my hands full over here." Charlotte swiveled back to Annie. "Let's get started," she said with relish, advancing on a rack of glittering evening gowns.

She rummaged through them, hangers shooting across the rack. "Hmm," she murmured. "No, not that one.... Here, try this."

She held up a swirl of silk, but all Annie saw was the startling color—hot pink. She shook her head emphatically. "I couldn't possibly wear that," she declared. "I usually stick to dark blues."

Charlotte propped her elbow on the rack and subjected Annie to another thorough perusal.

"I'm going to give you some advice," she said. "Don't wear navy blue anymore. Trust me on that."

Somehow Annie ended up in front of a mirror, her body wrapped in hot-pink silk. She felt like a neon sign! But then she looked ... and looked again, staring at herself in complete surprise.

Her hair was dark and lustrous in contrast to the unabashed pink of the dress; her skin glowed with a soft rose. The neckline, falling in a dramatic V, exposed more skin than Annie was used to seeing. The dress had short cap sleeves, although the gored skirt swooped to ankle length. It was a dramatic style, one that made Annie look slender and voluptuous at the same time. She closed her eyes for a minute. When she opened them, her reflection leapt out at her again—vibrant, glowing, alive.

"Can that be me?" she exclaimed.

Charlotte grinned. "It's going to be the new you. What do you say?"

Annie lifted her shoulders, feeling the silk move sensuously with her body. Something reckless and daring was taking over her normal caution. She didn't even ask how much the dress cost.

"I'm going to wear it tonight," she declared. But Charlotte was moving on to other matters, picking out a pair of black pumps from her shoe display.

"These will be just right . . . and ultrasheer hose, of course. Now we've done the easy part." She waited for Annie to change back into her ordinary navy blue, then started brandishing a hairbrush.

"Head down," she said.

"What—" But before she could get any more words out, Annie found herself leaning over and staring at the floor, her hair hanging upside down while Charlotte vigorously wielded the brush on it. Annie's scalp began to tingle. When she was finally allowed to straighten up, her hair stuck out wildly and crackled with electricity. Charlotte used a few deft strokes of the brush, taming things down a bit, yet keeping Annie's hair swept away from her face.

"You think your forehead's too high, don't you?" Charlotte asked. "Sure, it's high," she went on, "and wide, too. Shows you have brains! So don't try to hide it anymore under all those bangs. Flaunt it. I mean, look at me. See all these freckles?"

Annie nodded. There was a generous smattering of them across Charlotte's large nose and cheeks.

"I used to hate them," Charlotte explained. "I tried every darn thing I knew to cover them up. But now I figure they're sort of a trademark—just like the way I change my hair color every January first. See what I mean?" She didn't give Annie a chance to answer, but dragged a chair in front of a mirror. "Sit," she said.

Annie sat. Meanwhile the young redhead named Beverly rushed in from the street again and hurried over to Charlotte.

"I got everything you wanted," she said breathlessly, holding up a white plastic bag that read: Plaza Pharmacy.

"Good work, Bev." Charlotte took the bag and shook it out into Annie's lap. Small jars and compacts tumbled out, along with lipstick tubes and a mascara wand. Annie was skeptical about wearing all this stuff. Charlotte herself was resplendent in bold copper eye shadow and wine-red lipstick, but how would Annie look with a similar make-up job?

Charlotte pushed up a stool so that she could perch beside Annie. "Eyebrow pencil," she said. Annie hunted through the items in her lap and handed Charlotte the pencil. Two customers had come into the store and were looking on with interest. Annie shifted uncomfortably in her chair. She didn't like being the center of attention.

"Hold still, or you'll have eyebrows where you never knew before," Charlotte said good-naturedly. "I'm going out with my own boyfriend tonight. There's nothing like a nice, old-fashioned date, is there?"

"Actually, what I'm doing tonight isn't a date," Annie felt compelled to explain. "It's more like a business arrangement."

"You wear that dress and it'll be a date. Eye shadow next, and have the mascara ready." Charlotte's fingers moved with amazing dexterity despite the incredibly long nails, which were painted deep red, exactly

the shade of her dress and lipstick. They flashed back
and forth in front of Annie's eyes. "Just another
touch there.... All right, now for the lipstick," Charlotte announced. "No, not that shade. It's too quiet.
Give me the other one—that's it." A few moments
later she slid the stool away and observed Annie with
satisfaction. "Not bad. Not bad at all. Aren't you
going to look at yourself?"

Annie forced her head to turn toward the mirror,
and once again she was surprised by the sight. She
didn't look made up at all; Charlotte had used only a
light smudge of eye shadow in a gentle mauve. It
blended in subtly with the tone of Annie's skin, high-
lighting her dark eyes. The mascara was expertly applied, lengthening Annie's already thick lashes, and
the lipstick merely deepened her lips' natural shade.
The lush contours of her mouth were neither suppressed nor emphasized; they were allowed simply to
be what they were. Altogether the effect was more so-
phisticated and at the same time more natural than
Annie's own perfunctory efforts with makeup had ever
been.

"I like what you did," she said. "You're awfully
good at this."

"I know," Charlotte said complacently. "But the
important thing is to learn how to do it yourself. I
want you to take it all off with that cold cream, and
we'll start over. And this time you'll do the work."

Annie's hands were used to fine detail. With a little
prompting it didn't take her long to recreate the look
of natural sophistication. Charlotte nodded in ap-

proval. By now the other customers had drifted away, but she lowered her voice when she spoke to Annie.

"You do a few other things before this big date of yours, and you'll be a smashing success. Of course, you've got to do what I tell you in the right order, so you can work yourself up to the finale. I'm talking about my trade secret for success—that'll be the finale. Now, first of all..."

Some time later Annie's head was whirling with Charlotte's instructions and her arms were piled high with boxes and assorted packages. She stood in the doorway of Carlotta's, saying goodbye.

"Thank you for everything. It was really very kind of you..."

"It was fun." Charlotte grinned at her. "Maybe I'll branch out into a whole new line of business. 'Makeovers by Carlotta.' How does that sound? Be sure you knock him off his feet tonight!"

And with that Annie was launched back into the outside world, striding off to find Derrek.

CHAPTER EIGHT

"YOU LOOK DIFFERENT," Derrek said when he saw her a few moments later. Thoughtfully he stowed all her purchases in the Jeep. Annie smoothed the collar of her blouse, hoping her make-up job still looked good.

"What do you mean, different?" she asked.

"I don't know. I can't decide yet." He studied her, rubbing his jaw. "You look like you haven't brushed your hair," he said at last.

"Thanks a lot."

"You should not brush your hair more often." He smiled at her, a tender, whimsical smile, and Annie felt her heart speed up.

She was silent on the ride back to the house; so was Derrek. As soon as they arrived, she sequestered herself in her room. She felt as if she'd started a snowball rolling the moment she'd walked into Carlotta's, and now the snowball was tumbling along, getting bigger and bigger all the time. She didn't know how to stop it—or if she wanted to stop it. She took her notepad out of her purse and read over what she'd scribbled. Charlotte's instructions, her "trade secrets."

"I've never taken a bubble bath in my life," Annie muttered, frowning at her notes. She poked about among the packages arrayed on her bed and found one of the white plastic bags from Plaza Pharmacy. Annie fished out the jar of bubble bath and read the label. Then she shrugged and dumped a goodly portion into the bathtub, faucets on full blast, creating a froth that began to drift over the sides.

Annie lowered herself gingerly into the tub, feeling much too self-indulgent. But when she leaned back, she was able to relax for the first time all day. The combination of steamy water and fragrant bubbles was soothing. She wiggled her toes and allowed her eyelids to drift closed. When she emerged it was with reluctance. She followed the luxurious bath with her usual brisk shower so she could wash her hair.

Shivering a little in her cotton robe, a towel wrapped around her head, she consulted her notepad again. Goodness, next she was supposed to treat her skin with lotion and powder. Annie felt as if she were seasoning herself like a roast for Sunday dinner. She smoothed on the lotion, puffed on the powder and advanced down the list to coral-pink nail polish.

By the time she reached the last item, Annie was frazzled. She was scented and softened and polished in every way possible. Her makeup had been carefully reapplied; her hair was thick and full of body, swept away from her face again. According to Charlotte, it was at this point that Annie should be brimming with energy.

"Because now we've come to the most important thing," Charlotte had proclaimed. "Your attitude! You just go out there tonight and believe in yourself. It's a matter of projection, you know what I mean? You project what you want to be, how you want people to look at you. Make a picture of yourself in your

THE TURQUOISE HEART 119

mind and send it out. But you've got to be intense about it or it won't work. That's my secret for success."

Right now Annie didn't feel like projecting even the soggiest image of herself. She rustled about the room in her hot-pink gown and thought with longing of the black dress, which would have permitted her to blend right into the background. She gazed bemusedly at the two pairs of madras shorts she had draped over a chair back.

Derrek knocked on the door. "Annie, are you ready to leave?" he called.

"Yes . . . no!"

"Which one is it?" he asked from the other side of the door.

"I'm almost ready," she amended. As if it would somehow give her strength, she hurried over to the bureau and picked up the turquoise pendant. Fastening the chain around her neck, she saw that the stone was a vivid but pleasing contrast to the pink dress. It nestled provocatively just at the spot where her breasts began to swell, only slightly hidden by the folds of her neckline. Annie took a deep breath, went to the door and flung it open.

Derrek gazed at her for a long moment without saying anything. Annie felt herself knotting up inside. Now everything seemed wrong—the bright dress, the hair swept boldly away from her face, the tropical jasmine perfume. She told herself frantically that she could wear her navy-blue suit instead. She'd change into it and comb her hair back over her forehead—

"You look so beautiful, Annie." Derrek's voice was husky. He took a step toward her, capturing both her hands in his. The blue of his eyes was very dark and intense as he continued gazing down at her. "You always look good to me, but tonight you shine."

Annie smiled a little, for she didn't feel confident of her looks at all.

"Thank you," she said gruffly. He cradled her hands against his chest. Without thought or reason she moved closer, letting her cheek brush against his. She stayed next to him like this for a moment, breathless, aware of the pulse beating in her throat. Then she moved her head until her lips found the corner of his mouth. He made no response of his own, waiting for her, tantalizing her to go on and take the lead.

"Derrek," she whispered. "Kiss me." He turned and his mouth took possession of hers. He courted her with a gentle kiss. The sweetness of it pierced her, and yet she wanted more from him—she wanted his passion. But then Derrek stepped away from her and regarded her intently. She was trembling, her breasts rising and falling under the thin silken material of her dress. She could not look into his eyes.

"Annie . . . you're still afraid to admit that something's happening between us."

"That's not it at all," she countered. "I know perfectly well that something's happening."

"We're making progress, then." His tone was light and teasing, but Annie couldn't be lighthearted in return.

"We both need to stop this," she declared. "We're rushing into things and we don't know each other at all yet."

"I guess we'd better hurry up and get to know each other, then." Laughter simmered just beneath his voice.

Annie bit her lip. She felt too many conflicting emotions whenever she was with Derrek. "You're crooked," she said briskly. He was wearing a tuxedo, and his cummerbund was twisted. She reached out and straightened it with a tug here, a pull there. "That's better. You don't look so bad yourself tonight." She kept her tone matter-of-fact.

"I hate this damn suit," he said, shrugging impatiently. "Feels like I'm wearing a straitjacket." The rick dark cloth of the tuxedo offset his black hair; its excellent cut accentuated his tall rangy frame. He looked both elegant and rakish. But he seemed uncomfortable, as if he couldn't wait to get back into his blue jeans. It made Annie feel more confident to know that she wasn't the only one suffering tonight. She slipped the strap of her new mesh evening bag over her shoulder.

"I'm ready," she announced. "Shall we go?"

Together they walked outside. The Jeep had been given a wash and its top was snapped into place.

"I always put the top up for special occasions," Derrek explained. Annie smiled at him in spite of herself. Derrek could surely afford to buy any car he wished, but he drove only a rugged Jeep. She liked that. This time she waited for him to help her up into the seat, holding on to her long skirt while he grasped her firmly around the waist. His touch was very warm through the flimsy silk. Then he swung aboard his own side and started the engine. They began jouncing down the drive.

Annie felt a coldness settle inside her as she remembered that the evening ahead was, in fact, a test. More than anything else, she had to prove herself to Derrek.

A short while later, they pulled up at a startling hulk of adobe and brick that looked like a cross between an English manor house and a Spanish fortress. The mansion loomed on a hill covered with sagebrush and juniper trees, overlooking the sparkling lights of Santa Fe spread out below. Annie climbed the stone steps to the massive front door, her hand gripping Derrek's arm.

"Attitude," she muttered to herself. "Projection!"

"What was that?" Derrek asked.

"Um, nothing." Annie lifted her head as the massive door opened silently in front of them. She made one last desperate effort to project an image of herself: Annie Brooke, museum director. Charming, gracious, witty—life of the party! Oh, hell. She had never understood the necessity for these social functions, but tonight her dreams were on the line. She dug her fingernails into Derrek's arm, her whole body tense as they crossed the threshold. A butler bowed to them with a flourish of tails. He had a bald head that shone immaculately in the light cast by a crystal chandelier.

"Your wrap, madam?" he asked in a deep rumbling voice.

"My...oh, I didn't bring one," she told him. "It's really quite warm outside, and I didn't think I'd need a coat or anything like that. Of course, later on it might get chilly—"

Derrek propelled her onward. *Get control of yourself. No more babbling!* Annie instructed herself firmly. That had been an unexpected attack just now. Derrek began introducing her around, and she was careful only to nod and smile politely. But there were too many faces and they began to blur, dissolving into a glitter of jewelry and teeth. That was all she could seem to focus on—people's teeth. She was definitely going to have a problem later, trying to match names and faces with sets of molars. How she hated being dropped into the middle of a crowd like this!

She kept hold of Derrek; he was her one anchor. But then he loosened himself from her grip.

"You're on your own now," he murmured. "Remember, act like a museum director."

"Derrek!" she croaked, but he'd already disappeared into the crowd. Annie glanced around to see what kind of position he had left her in. She was on the edge of a small group, and the conversation had something to do with rising land values in Santa Fe. Annie tried to look interested in the subject, and found her jaw clenching with the effort. As she understood it, the way to socialize was simply to wait for an opening in the conversation, and then jump in. She really began to listen now.

"Of course, the real-estate market has never been better," said a woman in a long dramatic skirt of black leather. "Santa Fe is attracting all the right people. Just the other day I sold a house to Linea Martin. She's tired of Beverly Hills."

"I wish I could be impressed by your little coup," said a portly man in a bored tone of voice. "Linea Martin is a mediocre actress at best."

"Who cares if she can act?" retorted the woman, sounding annoyed. "The point is, she paid a stupendous price for a three-bedroom adobe. Now values in the whole neighborhood will skyrocket and I'll get the best commissions of my career."

"It's a disturbing trend, don't you think?" Annie asked, seeing her chance to jump in. Faces swiveled around to look at her, but she plunged ahead. "The same thing has happened in other towns—wealthy people moving in and driving up the prices. And then the people who've lived in those towns all their lives have to struggle just to pay property taxes."

The woman in black leather stared at her. "Are you in real estate?" The woman's eyes bored into her. All those faces were looking at her, examining her. Annie felt like a laboratory specimen under analysis. She cleared her throat forcefully.

"Um, no, I'm not."

"Real estate is *my* field of expertise," pronounced the woman. All the faces obligingly swiveled in her direction, and she went on with a self-important air, "When land values go up, everyone wins. It's the best possible thing for the entire community."

"Rich people win," Annie persisted. "Poor people lose." The faces swiveled back to her.

The woman in black leather looked annoyed, and abruptly she changed the subject. "Now, before I was interrupted," she said pointedly, "I was going to tell the most amusing story about Linea—"

"You're going to give us the condensed version, I hope," said the portly man with the bored voice. Now the woman in black leather was glaring at him, not at Annie. The faces had swiveled around to watch him.

Annie's contribution had sunk into the conversation like a stone in water; not even a ripple was left on the surface. She was quite happy to leave that group and position herself alone by a large mullioned window. It was a good observation post.

The party was taking place in an immense room with a cathedral ceiling. Several paintings and Oriental rugs decorated the walls, but Annie imagined the place would seem cavernous with all the people gone; it wasn't suited for anything but a large crowd. She scanned the room, unconsciously looking for Derrek. He wasn't far away, standing in the midst of another group. But instead of joining in the conversation, he was watching Annie sardonically. She straightened, returning his gaze coolly. Then she started making her way to the other side of the room.

She came to an alcove where four musicians were performing a lilting Mozart quartet. Annie stood against a wall and listened to each movement of the piece. She enjoyed watching the musicians. The first violinist was a teenage boy who played with his eyes closed. He leaned into the music, lank hair falling over his forehead. His wide mobile mouth opened and closed depending on the intensity of the passage. Once in a while he smiled to himself, as if a certain phrase made him especially happy. When the last note faded away, his bow remained on the strings, quivering into stillness. Slowly he opened his eyes and looked around. His expression was forlorn, as if he wanted the music to go on forever.

Annie approached him. "That was wonderful," she said, still caught up in the Mozart, too. He pushed his hair back, but it promptly fell over his forehead again.

"Thank you, ma'am," he said. "Sometimes we don't know if anyone is listening to us at these parties."

Annie suspected it wouldn't matter to this boy if anyone was listening or not; he obviously loved what he was doing. As the musicians began to play again, she gravitated to the large buffet table. She picked up a plate and began to serve herself some avocado salad. Derrek appeared beside her and picked up a plate of his own. They were isolated here together, at one end of the long table.

"You've really been circulating," he said dryly.

"I'm still making the rounds," Annie responded. She studied the lobster mousse and the stuffed artichoke hearts.

"Annie, you're supposed to actually talk to people at a party like this."

"Seems to me that's exactly what I've been doing. I've been socializing." She concentrated on the miniature quiches. Who made pie tins that small? And each tiny pie crust was perfectly fluted around the edges. "Fascinating," Annie murmured. She gave herself one and plunked another on Derrek's plate for good measure. He piled some cheese puffs next to it.

"Your idea of socializing is talking to the musicians and then going off to eat by yourself," he told her. "That's just not good enough."

Annie slapped a piece of cranberry bread onto her plate. "I also participated in a very interesting conversation about real estate," she declared.

"Yes, I overheard. You were inept, and that's putting it kindly. You managed to insult every rich person in the room. Now tell me how you plan to ask them for contributions after that.'' He paused. ''I'm more skeptical than ever about you being director of the museum.''

She jabbed at a slice of prosciutto with her fork. She wouldn't let herself listen to him. ''I'm the person for that job, Derrek,'' she said tightly.

''You still haven't proven that to me.''

''Look,'' she exclaimed. ''I'll tell you what the problem is here. It's not me. It's these stupid fund-raisers! No one gets any fun or enjoyment out of them. Whoever really wants to make a contribution should just write out a check and put it in the mail. That would save everybody a lot of time and aggravation!'' Triumphantly she popped a cherry tomato into her mouth.

Derrek was implacable. ''It just doesn't work that way, Annie. Hell, I don't enjoy these things any more than you do. But people have to be charmed into giving away their money. If you can't learn how to do that, you're not the person for the job.''

Frustrated and angry, Annie strode away from the table. But she knew she wouldn't be able to escape Derrek. He would be watching her, judging her every move and finding it lacking. She sat down on the edge of a Chippendale side chair, trying to look as if she was part of the particularly noisy group beside her. Without enthusiasm she poked at the food on her plate. It was delicious and yet her appetite had completely disappeared.

A vague bustle of activity was taking place at the front of the room. Annie craned her neck to see what was going on. A thin elderly woman had climbed onto a dais with the assistance of the butler. She was wearing a gown so heavily beaded it looked as if it could stand up by itself. Her hair looked heavy, too, an elaborate arrangement of white curls piled on top of her head.

The woman rapped a gavel on a podium. "Ladies and gentleman," she intoned, "we are here tonight . . ." Her frail voice was lost in the clamor of the room, and Annie strained to hear it. ". . . the Richards Foundation and in memory of our dear Carlisle Richards . . ." Annie gave up trying to hear the speech, and apparently so did everyone else. The hubbub rose again like a recording turned to full volume.

"This is excellent cranberry bread," Annie said loudly to no one in particular. But she was like the beaded lady at the podium, and received no attention at all.

The gavel rapped sharply again. "Time for our auction . . ." said the woman. "Proceeds go to the Richards Foundation . . . exquisite diamond earrings donated by . . ." Her voice sank once more. The woman herself seemed to be sinking a bit lower under the weight of her dress and her hair. The exquisite diamond earrings up for bid were nowhere to be seen, although the beaded lady appeared to be clutching something in her hand. She banged the gavel with her other hand.

"Do I hear five hundred . . ." Mumble mumble.

Several people became caught up in the spirit of bidding as soon as they realized an auction was in progress. General confusion ensued, but the beaded lady kept doggedly to her path regardless of what was happening in the audience. The gavel came down with surprising force, the earrings went to a gentleman who had already been outbid, and the butler appeared with the next article to go on the block—an impressive inkstand in ebony and ormolu.

Against her will, Annie's eyes sought out Derrek. He was leaning against a wall, frowning down at his cheese puffs. He stood solitary and apart, although he'd complained about Annie's desire to do the same thing. She couldn't tolerate this anymore—pretending that she knew how to be a social success. It wasn't even something she wanted to be. And yet her dreams depended on it!

She felt as if she would choke on her food. Standing up, she put her plate down on the first flat surface she encountered. All she longed for was a temporary respite from this senseless party, and then she'd be ready to do battle again. She moved quickly along one of the walls, as far away from Derrek as she could get. Somewhere there had to be a bathroom or another quiet place. Reaching a door, she pulled it open and went through without looking to see where she was going.

She stumbled over the first step of a carpeted stairway. Pulling the door shut, she gathered her skirt and hurried up the stairs. The din of the party was left behind her, hushed until it was only a faint murmuring. She emerged into the dimness of a wide hallway, with one light glowing from a wall bracket. Her heels sank into the deep-pile carpet as she searched for a bathroom. She found one that was bigger than the living room of her Denver apartment.

Annie gazed at the huge Roman tub, the expanse of tile spreading out before her, the yards and yards of shower curtain. Everything about this house was so big and impersonal! She went to the mirror that stretched above three sinks. Her eyes seemed too big and dark in her face, especially with her hair swept back. All the angles of her face were exposed, but Derrek had said she looked beautiful.

Annie turned on a faucet at one of the sinks and ran cool water over her hands. She wanted to splash her face, too, but that would mean disturbing her make-up and getting water spots on her dress. She felt brittle, as if she couldn't move or speak with any freedom at all. Right now she would welcome some old faded jeans like Derrek's.

Out in the hallway again, Annie debated how long she could stay up here. She drifted down the hall, away from the stairs. And then she heard a muffled sound behind one of the closed doors. Someone was weeping.

Annie's first impulse was to retreat quickly and quietly. Grief was a private thing and she didn't want to be caught intruding. It was also a messy thing, getting involved in other people's problems, and Annie wasn't ready for that tonight.

But she hesitated; the weeping sounded so disconsolate. Before she could give herself any time to think about it, she raised her hand and tapped on the door. Immediately the crying stopped.

"Are you all right in there?" she called softly. There was no answer, and now Annie knew that she couldn't turn back. She tapped once again on the door and opened it. She peered inside.

A young girl was sitting bolt upright in a bed, an afghan clutched protectively around her shoulders. Lamplight fell over the waves of her long brown hair.

"Who are you?" the girl demanded.

"I'm Annie. I came up to get away from the party, and I thought I heard something. But maybe I was mistaken," she added, giving the girl a chance to preserve her dignity.

"Don't you like parties?"

"Not especially."

"Well . . . you can come in if you'd like. I won't tell anybody you're here."

"I'd appreciate that." Annie stepped into the room. It was a cheerful place, with posters of rock stars and exotic animals tacked liberally on the walls. She stopped in front of a poster that showed a fuzzy koala bear clinging to the branch of a eucalyptus tree. She smiled as she glanced about, for the rock stars were definitely outnumbered.

"You like animals a lot, don't you?" she asked.

"I'm going to be a vet," the girl said. "My dad keeps telling me that the job market looks bad for veterinarians and why don't I go into marketing. But I know what I want to do. You can sit over there if you'd like."

Annie went to the battered rocking chair the girl pointed out. It was quite comfortable. She eased her toes out of her new pumps and flexed them gratefully.

The girl was probably no more than thirteen or fourteen. She had a long pointed face that just escaped being homely, and lovely dark gray eyes. Right now they were red-rimmed, and tears began to spring out of them.

"Oh, darn!" she exclaimed. "I keep thinking they'll dry up, especially if I let loose for a while. But I've let loose an awful lot tonight, and it hasn't worked."

The girl had a box of tissues beside her on the bed, but Annie fished in her evening bag and handed over a tissue of her own. The girl took it with a muttered thank-you and blew her nose.

"What's your name?" Annie asked after a moment.

"Beatrice. Can you believe my parents would name me something like that?"

"Yes, I can," Annie said. "My parents named me Annabel."

"Oh, well, that's not as bad as Beatrice," the girl said generously. "You can call yourself Anne or Annie, but the best I can do is Bea." Tears leaked from her eyes and she dabbed at them. "I'll be all right in a minute," she said, not sounding hopeful.

"Would you like to talk about it?" Annie asked.

Beatrice was silent for a while, nose buried in a tissue, but then she lifted her head.

"Maybe it would help to talk," she said. "It's about Mark Randall. He is—was—my boyfriend. The first I ever had, and things were going really great until Linda Casey decided to make a play for him. It figures, doesn't it? Mark and Linda sounds so much better than Mark and Beatrice."

Annie rocked slowly in the chair.

"Are you in love with Mark?" she asked.

"Yes," came the muffled reply. And now Annie didn't know what to say. There were all the usual things—"you're too young to be in love," or "you'll get over this before you know it." But Annie remembered too vividly what it was like to be a teenager, and couldn't say those things at all.

"Have you ever been in love?" Beatrice asked after another long moment.

Annie thought of Derrek, and her throat went dry. "I...I don't know," she said at last in response to Beatrice's question. "I really don't know." Her heart was beating too quickly.

"You're pretty enough. I guess a lot of men have been in love with *you*."

"I don't think so," Annie said wryly. "But I know that what you're going through isn't easy. There's nothing I can say to make it any better. Except...you're not afraid to love, and that's something you should be proud of."

Beatrice looked thoughtful and blew her nose again. Annie slipped her feet into her shoes and stood up.

"I'd better get back downstairs," she said. "I hope everything works out for you." Beatrice seemed awfully young, and Annie had a sudden urge to smooth her hair and tuck her under the covers. However, she sensed that restraint was needed here.

Beatrice sat up a little straighter. "Thank you for coming by," she said formally.

Annie walked to the door, but then leaned back into the room. "Have you ever thought of the name Trish?" she asked. "That could be short for Beatrice any day."

Beatrice tucked a strand of hair behind her ear, and slowly the corners of her mouth turned up. Her face looked winsome when she smiled.

"Mark and Trish...I like that. I like it a lot!"

Annie smiled back at her and gently closed the door as she went out. She had a good feeling that Linda of Mark-and-Linda might be in for some renewed competition.

Still smiling, Annie turned around and bumped smack into Derrek.

CHAPTER NINE

DERREK'S ARMS reached out to steady Annie, but she pulled away. Her smile faded.

"I don't believe it," she said angrily. "You even had to follow me up here. All right, I admit it, I was trying to get away from that wretched party. But I'm going back down there again. I'll do it right this time!"

She brushed past him, hurrying back to the noise and confusion downstairs. The beaded lady was still at work, stalwartly auctioning off a set of gilded silverware.

Derrek caught up to Annie as she was making her way toward the musicians again.

"Look," he said, taking her arm. "What do you say we just get out of this place? I think we've both had enough here for one night."

Annie looked around at the crowd of people and didn't argue with him. Outside the air felt cool and fresh on her skin. She had botched the evening, but she didn't want to hear about it, not another word. Derrek drove her back to the house and she headed straight for the haven of her room.

"Annie, wait. It's still early. Come to the patio and I'll bring you some wine."

She wanted to refuse him. He awakened so many conflicting emotions inside her—desire and delight, but also uncertainty and fear. And yet one emotion overwhelmed all the others—a craving for his nearness. It wasn't something logical Annie could explain or argue against. Without speaking she went out to the patio to wait for him.

The patio was actually an inner courtyard, surrounded on all sides by the house. She sank onto a wooden bench, leaning back against a picnic table. From here she could see through a window into the lighted kitchen. Derrek was rummaging in the cabinets, his jacket off and his sleeves rolled up. Even from here Annie could sense the energy coiled up in him tonight. Something tightened in her own body as she gazed at him, and she felt a longing she could not define. Then he came out to her, bringing two long-stemmed glasses of white wine. He sat beside her on the bench, and Annie sipped from her glass. A breeze rustled through the bushes.

"Annie, I was listening when you talked to Beatrice."

She stiffened. "Please, Derrek, don't start on me again—"

"Hear me out. I didn't mean to eavesdrop. The door was open, and I heard your voice. I followed you up there because I was worried about you—and fed up with you for running away from the party. You kept talking about how much you wanted that blasted job, and I was determined to have you face what the job really means." Derrek gave a wry laugh. "Then I heard you talking to Beatrice. You handled it just right, Annie. If you can do something like that, you've got all the people skills you'll ever need. I think I understand your problem better now. You seem able to have such empathy with one person at a time. All you have to do is make sure you don't lose that quality even when you're in a crowd."

Annie sat very still. His praise was important to her; she hadn't realized how badly she'd wanted to hear it. Other people had always believed her to be cold and unfeeling, but Derrek was telling her she wasn't like that.

"Oh, Derrek, I really need to do it. I need to get that job and succeed at it!"

"Well, I'll tell you another thing, Annie. You looked the part tonight, every inch of you." His finger grazed her cheek lightly. Annie turned toward him, but then he stood up with a restless motion. He left his glass behind and paced about the courtyard. Dry leaves scattered under his feet. It was a melancholy sound, harking back to autumn and winter.

"What does the *F* stand for?" Annie asked suddenly. Derrek looked back at her, a distracted expression on his face.

"What do you mean?"

"Your name, D. F. Richards. I just wondered—"

"It stands for Franklin," he said, a touch of irony in his voice. "That was my grandfather's name on my mother's side. And Derrek was a name my mother chose just because she liked the sound of it. My father didn't really care what I was named."

Annie set her own glass down. She felt an instinctive need to battle the bitterness in Derrek. "Maybe your father only wanted to defer to your mother's wishes."

"No. He just didn't care. It was as simple as that." Derrek paced again. "Lord, it rankles," he muttered.

"Going to these fund-raisers and meetings, and hearing his name all the time. Listening to everyone tell me what a great man he was. Tonight I could hardly stomach it."

Annie stood up, hugging her arms to her body. The breeze seemed too cold now. "Derrek, I know your father wasn't perfect, but no one is. Can't you leave it behind? Can't you forgive him?"

"I don't know," Derrek said harshly. "I've tried, but I don't know if I can ever forgive him for what he did."

He was making a brutal judgment, one that Annie would never make, not even on her own parents. Her father had abandoned her, her mother had hardly paid any attention to her. And yet she had to absolve them, at least try to understand them, or she could never go on with her life.

She looked at Derrek. He stood outlined in the light streaming from one of the windows, his profile intense and the elegant leanness of his body accentuated. In his white dress shirt and black trousers he might have passed for a Spanish nobleman from another era. More than ever Annie was aware of the dark tensions inside him. Something compelled her to speak.

"Derrek, you were the one who defaced the painting of your father, weren't you?"

"Yes." The single word was toneless, and he did not move.

"It was a cruel thing to do," Annie burst out. "Cruel for your mother."

"She'd already left for Boston when it happened. You don't need to worry about her—I spared her that, just the way I've been sparing her everything else."

"You're angry at her, too." The statement came out like an accusation. "You're so angry at both of them, Derrek. You have to stop!"

Now he came over to her, his features rigid as he stared down at her.

"I want to stop, but I can't," he said in a taut voice. "Almost every night the scene plays itself over and over in my mind. I wasn't there, but I know exactly what happened. That's worse than if I'd actually witnessed everything myself."

Annie searched his face, shaken by the torment she saw there. "Derrek—what was it?" she whispered. "What happened?"

He didn't answer for a long while, just standing there and gazing down at her. But then he began to speak, slowly and with difficulty.

"My father couldn't paint toward the end. I don't know why. My mother said it was because he just didn't believe in himself anymore. I can see how that might have happened. Underneath all his bombast, he was a very insecure man. His ego was so fragile that he could never withstand criticism of his art. That meant he couldn't learn or improve. He was a good artist, I believe, but not a great one. If he finally realized that about himself, it must have been terrible." There was a brusque compassion in Derrek's voice. He reached out and gripped Annie's hand, but didn't seem aware that he had done so. He went on speaking without looking at her. Now his words came in a rush, as if he were anxious to get them out.

"After finally seeing his own weaknesses, my father could have accepted them and struggled to become a whole person. I believe he could have found wholeness—humility along with a genuine tolerance for himself, instead of an inflated ego. It wouldn't have been an easy struggle, but it was at least one of the choices he had. He made another choice instead. My mother thinks it was done in a moment of despair, without premeditation. I think he planned it very carefully, to make the most effect. He couldn't give up his grandiose image of himself and he was determined to die the same way he had lived—making an impact no one would ever forget. Early one morning he went out to his studio, placed a gun to his head and shot himself."

Annie drew her breath in sharply. "The newspapers said it was an accident—that he'd gone out hunting by himself—"

"My mother couldn't live with the thought that anyone would know the truth. She begged the police, she begged me never to tell anyone. The Richards name gave her the influence she needed...so it became a hunting accident." Derrek's hand gripped Annie's even more tightly. "She was the one who found him, you see. The man she'd worshiped all her life. She went out to the studio and found him. That almost destroyed her, and she still can't face the reality of it. I think she's actually beginning to believe the story of the hunting accident...."

Derrek's fingers burned into Annie's skin, but his touch sent no warmth through her.

"You say he planned it all." Her lips were stiff as she spoke. "But that means he realized your mother would come out to the studio... How could he want to hurt her so much? I can't believe that part is true, Derrek!''

"He loved her as much as he could love anyone." Derrek sounded tired now. "I grant him that. But he was a man who understood effect. What better way for the tragic artist to die than to have his wife find him like that in his studio? And the note he left had just the right touch of melodrama—I'm sure he drafted it several times until he had something that would sound good in the newspapers. He didn't count on the fact that my mother would rob him of his grand exit. And I've been helping her all along. Ironic, isn't it?'' He paused but then went on, like a man who's weary but can't stop trudging along.

"After it happened, after my mother left for Boston, I went out to the studio and tried to clean things up. The portrait of my parents was hanging there on the wall, mocking me. My father had portrayed so blatantly how it was between them all those years—my mother in the shadows, adoring him. And now I was picking up the pieces for both of them. For a moment it seemed as if my father was looking at me from the painting and laughing at me. He'd made sure that *I* wouldn't forget him. But even when I took the paint and blotted out his face, there was no forgetting.''

Silence drifted down like an added darkness. The light streaming through the windows into the courtyard could not dispel the shadows cast by Derrek's words. Annie began to shiver in the cool breeze, and he released her hand abruptly.

"You'd better go inside," he said. "I tried to tell you all along, Annie, that this wasn't a story for you.

It's not something tidy and clean." His eyes were bleak. Bleak and cynical. "Go," he said, his voice growing angry. "I need to be by myself right now."

"But, Derrek—" She reached out to him.

"Dammit, I need to be alone," he said harshly. Annie longed to comfort him, but it was no use. In his pain he had erected a barrier against her, hard and unyielding.

She turned and slowly left the courtyard.

THE SUNLIGHT SEEMED PALE and listless the next morning, drained of spirit. Annie was dressed in her usual subdued clothes—navy slacks and a nondescript beige blouse that washed all the rose from her cheeks. She'd felt too bright in her pink dress, and now she felt too colorless. She didn't know where she belonged anymore.

Annie straightened from her work on the portrait, unable to concentrate on it. It was progressing rapidly. She was using a solvent today, touching it carefully to that streak of paint with a cotton swab. Most of Carlisle Richards's face was revealed to her.

It was a distinctive face, with blunt features and florid skin. Tufts of graying hair sprang back from his temples. His expression radiated energy and impatience; he seemed to be gazing at some point far ahead. But Carlisle had not attempted to minimize the pouchiness under his eyes, or the slight weakness in the shape of his mouth. Perhaps it was only his inner weakness that he had not known how to confront.

Annie set down her jeweler's loupe and went to curl up on the window seat. Carlisle Richards had been a talented but destructive man; his wife was a dependent woman who had lived her life entirely through him. Somehow, in spite of all this, Derrek had forged his own unique strength. But even a strong person needed help and comfort. He had not allowed Annie to give him either of those last night.

In her mind she saw Derrek's face. Tired, strained from the effort of carrying a burden alone. Annie slid off the wide window ledge. For too long now she had retreated from other people; in many ways she had justly earned the reputation of being cold and unfeeling. And yet Derrek had taught her to recognize her own capacity for warmth. Empathy and passion—he had told her that she possessed both of those qualities. She needed to learn how to use them, and now was the time to start. Dammit, she would help Derrek, whether he wanted it or not.

Her heart pounding, Annie left the workroom and went to look for Derrek. She knew he was here somewhere because the Jeep was still in the driveway. Quickly she searched the house, skirting all the piles of junk and old papers. In one room she saw men's clothing heaped on a bed—suits, vests, shirts. Derrek had talked about not knowing what to do with his father's clothes. Painful as the job might be, it was usually the widow who sorted through her husband's belongings. Derrek was trying so hard to protect his mother. In a way, Annie herself was helping with this task of protection. When she finished her work on the portrait, Derrek's mother would never know it had been defaced.

Annie turned and hurried through the rest of the house, her heels clicking on the wooden floors.

"Derrek," she called. "Derrek!"

He didn't answer, and she realized where he must be. Annie felt uneasy and had to force herself to go through the back door. Now her heels tapped on the brick walkway. The garden looked even wilder to her than it had the other day, the weeds threatening to choke the few remaining flowers. She quickened her pace, her shoes sinking into the moist earth as the brick path faded out. She went through the trees to Carlisle's studio. The gate was unlatched, the door standing open. She paused on the threshold.

Derrek was sitting with hunched shoulders at the desk, the drawers pulled open on either side of him. His head was bent and he was holding a shiny object in his hands. Annie hesitated, and then walked into the room. No sense of foreboding greeted her and today this seemed merely a dusty unused place. For Annie the past did not call out in this room as it must for Derrek. She wanted to help him, but didn't know how. She stood in the middle of the floor, determined not to leave and yet unable to move toward the desk.

"Derrek . . ." she murmured at last. He looked up and she saw the moistness in his eyes, the lines of strain, more deeply etched than ever. She took a step closer, still unsure how to reach out to him.

Derrek spoke, his voice thick and unsteady. "I found this just now, stuck way back in one of the drawers of my father's desk." He held up a small trophy shaped like a cup. "I won this the year I was on the debating team in junior high school," he said as he turned it in his hands. "I was so proud of myself, bringing this home. I thought my father never gave a damn about it, but he kept it here in his desk all these years. It would have been so much simpler if once, just once, he'd told me he was proud of me.''

Annie moved another step closer. ''But he did keep the trophy,'' she said softly. ''That tells you he cared about you, doesn't it?''

Derrek bent his head again. ''I want to believe that,'' he said, so low that Annie could only just hear him. ''After all this time, I don't know if I can.''

She took the last few steps toward him, kneeling beside his chair and bringing her arms awkwardly but fiercely around him.

''Oh, Derrek, he loved you as much as he could. You have to believe that!'' She held him for a long while, but he didn't respond. ''Derrek, don't you see what's happening?'' she asked urgently. ''You'll never be able to resolve your feelings about your father this way—going through his things, trying to clean up what he left behind. That's what you've been trying to do for months, and it's not working. You know why? Because it's not your place to do all that. It's your mother's job. She's the only one who can do it.''

He kept his face turned away. ''I can't ask her to do it, Annie. She's been through enough already.''

''Derrek, listen to me,'' she said. It all seemed so clear to her now; she had to make him see it, too. ''Your mother will never have any peace until she comes back and does the job that's waiting for her. That doesn't mean just sorting through your father's clothes. Carlisle Richards was her life. If that's going to mean anything, doesn't she have to carry on for him? Doesn't she have to make some sense out of the tragedy? Think about it, Derrek! *She* should be the one taking over the foundation, honoring the man she loved but for once having some power of her own. For her it wouldn't be a travesty. It would be the fulfillment of her entire life. You've got to tell her that!''

Annie didn't know if her words were reaching Derrek at all. Her gave no answer to her impassioned plea. But then he set the trophy down on the desk and put his arms around her, holding her with his own fierceness. He leaned into her and she welcomed his weight gladly. She knew she had the strength to comfort him.

IT WAS TIME for Annie to leave New Mexico. She snapped her suitcase shut and looked around. The antiques Derrek had dragged in that first day were thoroughly dusted; the bed was stripped of its sheets, the Indian blanket folded on the mattress. Even the bathroom was sparkling, the sink and the tub carefully wiped. The place was far cleaner than it had been when Annie arrived. That was the mark she was leaving in this house—her habitual order and cleanliness. But it wasn't enough.

She wandered restlessly around the bedroom, wishing she could leave some other stamp of herself. So many emotions had awakened inside her these past few days. Surely they had made an imprint! But the room seemed too empty and her footsteps echoed hollowly.

Annie grabbed her suitcase and went out to the living room. The portrait of Carlisle Richards and his wife was now hanging on the wall among the other paintings. Annie had removed all traces of damage. Using both scalpel and solvent, she had completed her work on the portrait and then reframed it. No one would ever be able to tell it had been defaced. Annie clenched the handle of her suitcase. She ought to feel proud of herself. She'd accomplished her painstaking work quickly and efficiently, and the results were very satisfactory. But Annie didn't feel pride or satisfaction, only a dull ache deep inside.

"Ready to go?" came Derrek's cheerful voice behind her. She whirled around, trying to arrange her features in a businesslike expression. But the pain inside her sharpened to a knife point. She was leaving today, and yet Derrek seemed so happy!

He stood there in his faded jeans, thumbs hooked casually in his belt loops. His old cotton shirt of blue plaid accentuated the deep vivid blue of his eyes. The hair curling at his forehead added to his carefree look, and the lines of tension in his face were gone.

Derrek's mood had been subdued and thoughtful ever since he'd found the trophy in his father's desk. He and Annie hadn't talked much since then, exchanging only a few polite words when they met in the kitchen for meals. A constraint had fallen between them, but this morning Derrek appeared to be lighthearted and unaware of any tension. Annie felt it, though, a tautness thrumming in the air like a plucked violin string.

"I have everything packed," she said in a stiff tone. "It was kind of you to arrange a flight for me out of Santa Fe."

"It wasn't any trouble at all," Derrek answered, smiling at her. "Why should you have to go all the way down to Albuquerque to catch a plane? This way you'll be in Denver before you know it."

"That's good." She said the words automatically, without meaning. Annie reminded herself that she hadn't wanted to come to New Mexico in the first place. She should be glad that her business had been accomplished here so promptly. Now she could get back to the museum where she belonged. But why didn't Derrek *say* something? At least he could tell her that he was sorry to see her go. Instead he began whistling as he carried Annie's boxes of equipment to the Jeep.

She lifted her suitcase in beside the boxes and turned to look at the house one last time. Sunshine bathed the rambling adobe walls with a golden light. The vines climbing up to the roof were a healthy springtime green, thriving in spite of neglect. Annie still felt drawn to this place, even though she now knew about the unhappiness and bitterness that had taken root here. It wasn't the house's fault, and surely someday happiness would flourish behind those walls.

Annie climbed into the Jeep, pulling down her navy skirt with a yank. She had combed her bangs over her forehead and firmly curled under the edges of her long pageboy. She could imagine Charlotte giving a disapproving shake of her own wild yellow mane. But Annie felt more comfortable and secure with her old hairstyle. And she needed some security right now. The turquoise heart swung on its chain around her neck, but she'd tucked it under her blouse so that it would be hidden. She began to wish she hadn't worn it at all. The coolness of the stone against her skin seemed to mock the tumult inside her. She wanted so badly for Derrek to take her in his arms; she wanted just as badly to retreat to the safety of her museum. She didn't know *what* she wanted! Annie clenched her hands in her navy blue lap and stared straight ahead as Derek started the Jeep.

He whistled all the way into Santa Fe, progressing through several Broadway show tunes. It was Derek who'd talked about something happening between himself and Annie. Now it seemed that the ''something'' hadn't held his attention for very long. She'd been wise to resist him, and she should have resisted him a whole lot more. It was going to be difficult to erase the memory of his lips on hers. Tears pricked at Annie's eyelids, and she held her head high so that the tears wouldn't come sliding out. Derek started whistling another one of those damn songs.

Once in Santa Fe he turned onto a wide road and eventually pulled into a small parking lot. The airport building rose gracefully, the observation tower somehow a fitting crown for the thick rounded walls of adobe. Inside the building Annie also found grace and beauty. The wooden ceiling beams were decorated in a simple pleasing design, and the chandeliers were rustic in black wrought iron. There were only a few wooden benches, carved in their own simple and graceful lines. Annie sank down on one of them while Derek went off to check on her flight. But she felt too restless to stay seated, and she scrambled to her feet again. It seemed to her that this building captured the timeless spirit of Santa Fe that she'd already come to love. And Derek . . . did she love him?

She'd been so careful not to ask herself that question, and yet it had sprung, uninvited, into her mind. But she didn't know how to answer it! Her insides were churning in a confusion of longing and fear. Now Derek was coming toward her with his easy stride.

"Everything's all set," he announced. "Your gear's stowed on the plane. It'll only be a few minutes until takeoff."

Annie stared at Derrek's blue plaid shirt. The cloth was very worn; obviously he wasn't going to give up that shirt until it was in shreds.

"I suppose this is goodbye, then." Annie's throat felt scratchy as she spoke. Derrek didn't answer, he simply stood motionless in front of her. She started to get angry and tilted her chin. "Well, Derrek," she went on crisply, "good luck with the foundation. I hope you work everything out. I'll say goodbye now and we'll be done with it."

He smiled down at her, sticking out his hand as casually as if he was bidding farewell to a virtual stranger. Annie felt the anger boil up inside her.

"Blast you, Derrek F. Richards!" she muttered. She grasped him by the shoulders, brought his head down to hers and kissed him. All the passion inside her poured into that kiss. Her hands moved to cup his face, her fingers memorizing the feel of him. Her eyes were closed, her lips parted, and she demanded a response from him. At last he gave her what she needed, his arms tightening around her. She pressed close to him, oblivious to the people scattered about the waiting room. Annie knew only the lean strength of Derrek's body next to hers, the heat of his mouth and skin. But it couldn't last forever—she was only deepening her own pain. With an inarticulate moan, Annie pulled back from him. She turned and walked quickly away, the tears in her eyes finally spilling over.

CHAPTER TEN

ANNIE WAS WANDERING BLINDLY in the direction of the boarding gate when Derrek caught up with her. He took hold of her arm and steered her outside the building.

"You were going the wrong way," he said.

She tried to shake him off. "You're ruining my exit, Derrek. I've already said goodbye." In the sunshine her tears were like liquid prisms dazzling her sight. She blinked furiously against them.

"You certainly did say goodbye," he murmured, bringing her close to his side. "But you could always tell me again."

"Can't you just let me go?" she demanded.

"Not unless you know how to fly an airplane by yourself," he answered, steering her over to what looked like another parking lot. But instead of cars, rows of small planes were lined up on the asphalt. Annie came to an abrupt halt.

"You said that you'd arranged a charter flight, Derrek."

"I never said that. You just assumed it."

"You let me assume it. What's going on here?"

Derrek had her in motion again, and she couldn't brake in her smooth-soled pumps. He maneuvered her

over to one of the small airplanes. It was painted
bright yellow, with the name Betsy spelled on the side
in garish purple letters. The plane had a big pointed
nose and two propellers that looked like pinwheels.

"She's great, isn't she?" Derrek said, patting the
side of the plane. "Betsy and I will get you to Denver
in no time."

Annie's face was burning with outrage and embarrassment. "I don't believe you did this to me," she
said, her voice shaking. "You deliberately let me believe that I was going off on some charter flight and
wasn't going to see you again. Then you let me kiss
you like that."

Derrek grinned. Annie's face burned hotter, until
she was sure she must look like a Christmas-tree light.
"You think it's funny, don't you?" she asked. "Playing some kind of game with me, trying to see just how
big a fool I'd make of myself. Well, I hope I satisfied
you."

Derrek's smile faded. He was serious and intent as
he gazed down at her. "So that's what you think—that
you made a fool of yourself because you showed some
emotion for me with your kiss. But I wasn't playing a
game with you, Annie. Yes, I let you assume a few
things, but only because you were so determined to
assume them. You didn't need much help from me.
You wanted to believe I'd let you go off without even
talking about our relationship."

"That's not true!" she protested. "I didn't want to
believe that. I was really hurt."

"Then why didn't you speak? Why didn't you shake me and demand to know what was going on between us?"

Annie stared at the yellow plane. "I don't know," she said. "I just assumed you'd lost interest."

"Look at me, Annie. Really look at me and tell me how you could believe something like that."

She couldn't look at him. After a moment Derrek touched a finger to her chin, raising her head gently. Her breath caught in her throat at the expression of tenderness on his face.

"Annie, I've been trying to force you to take a stand about our relationship. Maybe that's not fair, but you've always retreated from me, refusing to admit that something important is happening between us."

"But, Derrek, nothing is clear!" she burst out. "We're attracted to each other—yes, that's true—but what else do we know about this relationship?"

"I'm willing to take a chance on finding out what's next for us. We've shared so much already, and that means a great deal to me. I'd never walk away without letting you know that. And yet just now you were going to walk away from me without a backward glance. Does being safe mean that much to you?"

"Derrek—I don't know," she said miserably. "I just don't know anymore."

He studied her with a wry expression. Then he climbed onto the wing of the bright yellow airplane and opened the door. He held out his hand to Annie.

"Wait a minute," she said. "This Betsy looks like a banana with wings. Are you sure it can fly?"

"She may be old, but she's airworthy." Derrek reached down and grasped Annie's hand, hauling her unceremoniously onto the wing. This was even worse than getting into the Jeep, she thought, as her narrow skirt clung awkwardly to her legs, hitching higher with every movement. The next thing she knew Derrek had pulled her through the door into the cramped narrow cockpit. She sat down beside him with a thump and he reached across her to slam the door shut. She felt as if she'd been stuffed into a cardboard box. The dashboard in front of her bristled with all sorts of gauges. It didn't seem like a real airplane, even when Derrek started the engines and they made a grouchy roar in her ears. She was used to the high but muffled whine of jet engines. The way her seat vibrated now, she felt as though she was sitting right on top of a propeller. Derrek leaned forward and tapped one of the gauges with his finger. It took several taps before a needle jumped to life.

"There, that's better," he said.

Annie stared at the instrument panel with growing apprehension. "How long have you been flying?" she asked.

"I started lessons about a year ago. I took one look at Betsy, and I knew she and I belonged together. Of course, I haven't had much time to fly these last few months. I may be a little rusty," he added carelessly.

Annie's mouth went dry and she clenched her fingers around her purse strap. "Derrek, I don't want to do this!" she exclaimed, raising her voice above the rattle of the engines. He glanced over at her with a grin.

"What's the matter? Don't you trust me? Relax."
The plane began to taxi. Derrek was piloting with
something that looked like a chopped-off steering
wheel. All the controls in here seemed more fitting for
a video-arcade game, not an airplane.

"Derrek, let me out of here!"

"Just trust me, Annie. Sometimes you have to risk
putting your trust in someone else. Life means taking
risks."

"I'm taking one right now," she said grimly.

"Only because I'm forcing you to. Someday you'll
have to take the first step yourself, no matter how
much it frightens you."

He made her feel earthbound, as if she hurried
through life without ever looking up at the sky. Annie
was dismayed because she couldn't deny the truth of
this. Her natural inclination was to seek security before anything else.

She looked at Derrek. His face was so vibrant and
alive right now. He made her think of the daredevil
pilots who had risked everything to fly the earliest
planes. Derrek probably would have felt right at home
with them. In spite of herself, Annie was caught up for
a moment in the sense of adventure. She let go of her
purse strap and sat up straighter in her seat. With determination she gazed out the windshield. It was small
and narrow, as if Betsy were squinting instead of
opening her eyes wide. The plane gained speed as it
turned onto the runway, rolling smoothly along. This
really wasn't so bad, Annie decided.

Then Betsy's innards emitted several burps, and Annie's brief moment of confidence vanished. She twisted around in her seat.

"What was that?" she demanded.

"Don't worry, she's just settling in." Derrek seemed to be having a better time than ever, but Annie's skin went clammy. She gripped the edge of her seat.

"Derrek, let's just turn this thing around."

It was too late. Betsy was lumbering at a gallop down the runway like a cow that had just spotted a bale of hay. She didn't seem in any mood to turn around. Faster and faster she went, rocking madly. Then she made a lunge into the air—

"Oh, Lord!" Annie cried, and clamped her hands over her face.

"YOU CAN OPEN your eyes now," Derrek said. The laughter that ran under his voice was becoming a familiar sound for Annie. She huddled down on her side of the taxicab, still wallowing in relief at being out of that plane. The taxi rocketed along, caught up in the frenetic pace of Denver's freeways. Annie didn't care. She was on solid ground, and that was all that mattered.

"I've never seen anyone hold their breath all the way from Santa Fe, New Mexico, to Denver, Colorado," Derrek remarked. "That was quite a feat."

Annie frowned at Derrek, but his expression remained humorous. He kept turning her life upside down. It was impossible to know what was going to happen next with him, and that scared Annie even more than Betsy had.

The taxi made two lane changes without signaling and tailgated another car so closely it looked like it was being towed. The cabdriver hunched over the wheel as if that would give him more leverage in the traffic. Whenever he turned his head Annie could see he had a mild-looking face, but he muttered epithets at other drivers that made her toes curl. His inventiveness was truly impressive. By the time the cab had jolted to a stop in front of the Darcy Museum, Annie had several new words in her vocabulary.

Four stone urns squatted in hideous Victorian splendor at the base of the steps leading up to the museum. Annie herself planted moss roses in the urns every spring in an attempt to mitigate their ugliness. This year's roses were blooming in profusion, and the red brick of the mansion seemed to welcome Annie home. Carrying her suitcase, she ran up the steps, impatient to be inside and to see what had happened while she'd been gone. But most of all she was eager to share the museum with Derrek. She knew that as a trustee he'd been here before, but she was the only one who could show him how special it was.

He deposited her boxes of equipment in her office, then stood back to look around. Annie went to her desk and began sorting through the mail. She couldn't pay much attention to it, though, because she was anxious to see what Derrek thought of her room.

The walls were paneled in amber-brown wood and smelled faintly of lemon oil. Shelves covered two of the walls and were packed with all of Annie's favorite books. She had tomes on art restoration, worn copies of novels, oversize books on art history with glossy reproductions of paintings. She didn't have any paintings hanging on the walls, only two framed posters. One depicted Victorian ladies in bonnets and hoop skirts playing croquet on a lawn. The other was a reproduction of Frederic Remington's *Cowpuncher's Lullaby*; the cowpuncher sat astride his horse and raised his head to the moonlit night, singing to the cattle so they wouldn't stampede.

Derrek was giving the place a thorough perusal. Annie was so nervous that she stabbed herself with the letter opener.

"Well...do you like my office?" she asked at last, fiddling with the pottery bowl where she kept her paper clips.

"It looks just like you," he said. "Serious and reserved, but then there's an unexpected flash of color or something whimsical to catch your eye." He nodded toward a weather vane that Annie had mounted and put in a corner. A plump spotted hen carved out of wood perched on the weather vane. The hen wore a philosophical expression, as if resigned to the fact that it had been retired from active duty; sheltered indoors like this, it could no longer point its beak to show which way the wind was blowing.

Annie gathered her mail into a stack. "I don't think I have anything urgent here," she said briskly. "We have time to take a quick tour of the rest of the museum."

She led him to the exhibits on the second and third floors, where she carefully adjusted the temperature and humidity settings. To Annie any painting was like a living breathing creature in delicate health, and she would care for it as tenderly as a nurse would a sick patient. She turned down the lights over one exhibit. Paintings were so fragile that even prolonged heat from an electric bulb could harm them. Annie knew that she ought to check on the Carlisle Richards exhibit. But seeing the relaxed expression on Derrek's face, she decided to bypass the Richards Wing entirely.

They wandered through the museum. Annie noted that the display of nineteenth-century portraits was attracting a lot of visitors. She felt a glow of pride, for she'd worked hard to put that exhibit together. On the second floor she led Derrek through carved arches situated every few feet down a long hallway. The arches were so exuberant that they almost made complete circles before reaching the floor. With their gilt trim they were startling and a bit gaudy, and walking under them made Annie feel as if she was in a carnival fun house. She reached the last one and brought Derrek to the full-length portrait of Caroline Darcy hanging on the wall.

She and Derrek stood in front of the portrait. Caroline had been a tall, big-boned woman with a handsome face. In the portrait her dark hair was swept up and anchored in a simple bun on top of her head. She wore an unfrilled walking dress that had no bustle, and her solid waist was not pinched in by a corset. Her brown eyes were calm, but her strong features hinted at a forceful will.

Annie smiled. "Caroline looks so plain compared to this house she lived in. I think she was born into the wrong time and she didn't know quite what to do about it.''

"You really feel like you're carrying on for her, don't you?" Derrek asked. "You feel as if you're the modern woman she was meant to be."

Annie stuck her hands into the pockets of her skirt. She'd often imagined herself in the role Derrek had described—a descendant of Caroline Darcy, in spirit at least. But now Annie realized she wasn't nearly as adventurous as she needed to be for that role. If Caroline were living right now, she'd probably be chugging around the skies in her own Betsy. Annie's sense of inadequacy was uncomfortable and unwelcome. Before meeting Derrek, she'd always felt that Caroline was smiling down at her from this portrait in approval. Now the smile didn't look nearly so approving. Instead it seemed to be saying, "Annie, go out and live a little! Kick up your heels!"

Just then Mr. Bessler, the current director of the museum, came bustling along through the arches. He moved perpetually in a flurry of activity, his silver hair sticking out at odd angles and his eyes darting behind round gold-rimmed glasses. He didn't like to stay in one place for very long and was always leaving half-finished tasks in his wake. Now his attention zoomed in on Annie.

"Miss Brooke! I'm so glad you're back. I was hoping you could go with me to the Frawley house tomorrow. They're finally allowing us access to those Civil War papers."

Annie smiled with pleasure. "That's wonderful, Mr. Bessler. We'll really be able to put together a good exhibit now."

"Another thing, Miss Brooke. Paul Cooper is still complaining that he can't retrieve the seventeenth-century data base on his computer. He's making quite an uproar about it."

"I'll talk to Cooper first thing in the morning," Annie said decisively. "The man is acting like a prima donna, but I'll set him straight."

"Good, good." Mr. Bessler looked relieved. His gaze skittered over to Derrek.

"Mr. Richards, how good to see you—an unexpected surprise. Please let me know if I can do anything for you." Mr. Bessler rocked from one foot to the other like a sprinter being held back from the starting line. He seemed at a loss for words with Derrek and glanced about expectantly as if he could snatch something to say from the air. Apparently nothing was forthcoming. He looked vaguely disappointed. "Well, well," he muttered, and bustled off again.

Derrek regarded Annie. "Seems like you're already running the museum. In everything but name, that is. Maybe I've underestimated you, Annie Brooke."

"Maybe you have," she responded tartly, but she couldn't help grinning at him.

"Do you have time to show me your old mill building?" he asked.

"Of course!" Annie exclaimed. She led Derrek outside and across the abandoned lot. "Can't you just see this turned into a beautiful park?'' she asked him. ''Over there, that's where I want to have a playground, with a big sandbox and lots of swings. We'll have a rock garden, too, so we won't have to seed the whole place for grass.'' Her dreams came to life for her as she spoke, and in her enthusiasm she grabbed Derrek's arm when they reached the mill.

''Just look at it,'' she breathed. ''Isn't it wonderful?''

The long four-story rectangle of brick was a study in simplicity. A tall blackened smokestack jutted from behind, and symmetrical rows of windows ran the length of each story. The building was unembellished except for a few dormer windows stuck into the sloped roof as if in an afterthought. The building was actually more beautiful than the ornate Darcy mansion across the way.

''I have the key right here.'' Annie struggled with the ancient lock of the door. ''You know, Derrek, the real-estate people are eager to negotiate with us. They'd like to get this property off their hands. They're willing to give us a very favorable deal.'' She pulled him along, up a creaky staircase. ''This is where I want the classrooms. For the art classes, remember?'' She gestured expansively around, not paying any attention to the broken window panes or the rubbish scattered on the scarred floor. The place would be sunny with all these windows, and already she could see stools and easels arranged on new floors of gleaming tile. ''Downstairs, that's where the big exhibits will be. The first one's going to be on trains.''

Derrek laughed and swung Annie around to face him. "You're full of ideas and plans," he said. "They're bursting out of you."

"Do you like my mill, Derrek?" she asked earnestly. He put his arm around her and together they walked the length of the room. Derrek knocked on the walls.

"The construction seems sound. Too many of these old places get torn down when they could be restored. There would be a lot of work involved here...but, yes, I like your mill, Annie, very much."

She felt a deep contentment. "Just wait until you see the rest of it," she declared, pulling him up another flight of stairs. "Now, this is where we'll have the Old West exhibit. I haven't told you about that yet, have I...?"

DEREK BALANCED two bags of groceries in his arms and Annie carried a third one. Spending the afternoon traipsing around the museum and the mill building had given her a ferocious appetite. She heard her stomach growling, and from the glint of humor in Derrek's eyes she knew he'd heard it, too.

"We have enough food here to feed a football team," he commented as he followed Annie into her apartment. "Are you sure you don't want me to help you fix anything?"

"No, this is my treat," she said firmly. She allowed him to deposit the groceries on the kitchen counter, and then ordered him to stay in the living room.

As Annie moved around the kitchen, however, she felt self-conscious about Derrek's seeing her apartment. She never seemed to have time to decorate the place. The curtains in the living room were a sallow shade of tan and had come with the apartment. So had the furniture—a lumpy sofa and a very uncomfortable easy chair. Both the sofa and chair looked like rejects from a motel room. For the last couple of years Annie had been meaning to go out and buy herself a new couch, but somehow she'd never got around to it.

She was relieved when Derrek came into the kitchen to watch her. At least the wallpaper in here was pleasant, with its pattern of fruit baskets and teapots running up and down the walls.

"I don't cook very often," Annie said, cranking open a can of mushroom soup. "But this is definitely a special occasion."

Derrek leaned in the doorway, a slow smile spreading over his face. "Let's see...canned soup, frozen lasagna and ready-made coleslaw. What do you do when you *don't* have time to cook?"

Annie tossed the lasagna into the oven. "You'd be surprised how long a person can survive on a jar of peanut butter," she remarked, ignoring Derrek's grimace. "Now, do you want corn chips, potato chips or both?"

It turned out to be a very satisfying meal, at least in Annie's opinion. She noticed that Derrek ate everything she'd piled on his plate and even asked for a second mug of soup. Afterward they sat together on the lumpy sofa, a bag of chocolate-chip cookies on the coffee table in front of them. Annie leaned her head back with a contented sigh. It was dark now, and she'd turned on only the small lamp in the corner. With this mellow light, the room didn't seem quite so drab.

Derrek drew her close, and her head rested naturally in the crook of his shoulder. He handed her a cookie.

"Happy?" he asked her.

"Mmm...yes." She munched the cookie and nestled a little closer to him. She was surprised to find how safe and protected she felt with him tonight. Those weren't emotions she had come to associate with him. He massaged her shoulder and her eyelids drifted downward. She was getting cookie crumbs all over herself and she didn't even care.

When Derrek kissed her, his lips were gentle. She felt him smile against her mouth.

"It's like kissing a chocolate-chip cookie," he said. "Annie, I'm feeling pretty happy myself."

"That's good." She slipped her feet out of her shoes and experimentally poked a toe at one of Derrek's cowboy boots.

"Just look at us," he said intently. "We really have something special together. Marry me, Annie."

She froze. A moment later she struggled away from him, holding her half-eaten cookie in front of her.

"Derrek, what did you say? Never mind, I *heard* what you said. You can't be serious."

He grinned. "Of course I'm serious. I want to marry you."

She brushed the crumbs from her skirt distractedly. Her heart felt as if it was beating in her throat.

"Derrek, we've known each other for less than a week! Don't you think you're rushing things?"

He gathered her close again. "I love you, Annie Brooke." His voice was husky. "And I know you love me, too."

She rested her forehead against his shirt, still clutching her cookie. She tried to think through the pounding of her heart. "Derrek," she said carefully. "I'm not sure yet how I feel about you. It's too soon. I mean, it's only logical. We need to give ourselves more time before we make any decisions."

"You're afraid, Annie." He said it as a statement, not a question. She leaned back so that she could look at him.

"Of course I'm afraid!" she exclaimed. "What rational person wouldn't be about something like this?"

"I'm not asking you to be rational. I'm asking you to look into your heart and tell me what's there." His intense blue eyes challenged her. She twisted away and retreated to the other side of the sofa. And yet she found that she had to do what he asked. She had to look inside herself. Taking a deep breath, she nodded.

"All right, Derrek. I'll tell you what I'm feeling, not what I'm thinking." She closed her eyes. "I feel . . . confused. I'm very attracted to you, and I like you. I like you a whole lot, Derrek. And I've never been so scared in my life." The chocolate-chip cookie fell out of her hand, unheeded. "You're asking me to make the biggest decision of my life, and I just can't do it! Not this soon."

She opened her eyes and looked at him. His black hair had tumbled over his forehead, untamed by brush or comb as if all the life and energy inside him had to find an outward expression. Something constricted inside Annie. She didn't want to lose him. She knew that much—she couldn't bear to lose him.

"Derrek, I have a plan," she went on eagerly. "Just hear my solution to all this. We'll keep seeing each other. You know, dating, and that sort of thing. It'll be a little difficult since we live in different cities, but we'll manage it. And we'll let matters progress naturally, one step at a time."

"Why don't we draw up a feasibility study while we're at it?" Derrek asked. "We'll graph a fifty-year projection so there won't be any surprises." He crossed to kneel in front of her, then anchored a hand on each side of her waist. "Annie, I know you love me. I feel it in my gut and in my bones. I've always trusted my instincts and I wish you'd start trusting yours. Come back to Santa Fe with me tomorrow. We'll work out all the details later." His voice was so persuasive, his touch so warm. But Annie stiffened her body.

"I have a job, Derrek. Have you forgotten about that? You can't just ask me to leave it—"

"Take a vacation. Call Bessler tomorrow and tell him you're going on your honeymoon." He leaned close to her, his lips against the pulse at her throat. Involuntarily her hands went to his shoulders and she bent her head over his.

"It's not fair," she whispered. "You want me to give up everything. Stop being myself."

"No, I don't want that at all," he murmured. "I love the way you are. I even love the way you write thirty-page reports that no one can read. All I'm saying is that you need to take a risk now and then.''

She pressed her cheek into the vibrant silkiness of his hair. She stayed like that for a long moment, and then she stood up and stepped away from him.

"I'm needed at the museum, Derrek," she said. "Especially now that I have a chance to become director. I've worked so hard for that. You know about all the plans I have!''

"It's always plans and schedules with you, Annie." He, too, straightened up from the sofa. "You're hiding in that museum. Lord, you've been hiding there for years."

Anger flickered inside her. "That's how you see it," she said. "The museum means something very special to me. It's not just a job!''

"You're damn right it's not," he shot back. "You've made way too much out of that place. You've even turned it into your home! I can hardly believe you live in this apartment, Annie. You must have carted everything warm and personal over to your office. Why don't you just sleep there nights and make it official? You don't have anything else going on in your life.''

She dug her nails into her palms. "All I'm asking is for you to be reasonable, Derrek. Don't expect me to throw away everything I've worked for all this time.''

He studied her, his features tightening. "Maybe I've been wrong about you," he said in a stony voice. "I keep thinking you have emotion underneath all that control, but maybe you've trained yourself too well.

You aren't really capable of one spontaneous passionate action."

His words stung. They were much too cruel after the tenderness he'd given her tonight. He had reopened a deep wound—her fear that she would never be able to please a man. She held her arms stiffly against her body, determined not to show him that she was trembling.

"You want me to change everything for you, Derrek. My life, my work. All I need is some time to think, and you won't allow me that."

"I know what you'll do, Annie," he said quietly. "You'll come up with a safe tidy schedule that will keep me from getting too close to you. In the end, you'll think yourself right out of loving me. But that seems to be the way you want it."

He walked to the door. Annie stood imprisoned by her fear and anger, even though she longed to run to him. He looked back at her, as if waiting for her to do just that. Her resolve hardened. He was asking far too much of her! She stared at him, holding herself so rigid she felt as if her joints would snap. Derrek turned away from her.

"Goodbye, Annie Brooke," he said softly, and closed the door.

CHAPTER ELEVEN

A FEW WEEKS LATER Annie sat hunched at her desk in the museum. She gripped a pen and began writing forcefully on the budget form in front of her. She'd devised the form herself, with its five carbons and its myriad lines and boxes. Usually she filled out the lines with care, proud that she had invented something so complex and detailed, but today all she could hear in her mind was Derrek's mocking voice. "Brevity, Annie. Brevity."

Her pen tore right through the paper, down to the carbons. Damn! She couldn't stop thinking about Derrek no matter how hard she tried. Annie pictured his face, the way it looked when he laughed. He always put so much joy into his laughter, as if he had just been handed a gift.

Annie made an effort to concentrate. She straightened a pile of receipts that was already perfectly straight. Then she forced her pen to move down the budget form, neatly filling in the blank lines. She wondered how Derrek was doing at the foundation. He hated the work there so much. What he really needed was time to design houses, and time to work on his old shack in Madrid. The shack where he'd kissed her for the first time.

"Confound you, Derrek F. Richards!" Annie exclaimed out loud. She crumpled up her budget report and threw it across the room. It landed against the weather vane, and the spotted hen appeared to look at it with a puzzled expression. Annie buried her face in her hands, rubbing her eyes tiredly. It seemed so long since the night Derrek had walked out of her apartment and out of her life. She still wasn't any closer to understanding her feelings for him. They swirled inside her like a dark powerful storm. She could hardly eat; even her trusthworthy jar of peanut butter was going untouched.

Derrek had not written to her or even telephoned. One morning she had locked herself in the office and dashed off an impassioned letter to him. She'd told him exactly how unfair he was being. She had also told him how much those days in New Mexico had meant to her, and how terribly she missed him. Then she'd stood up and fed the letter into her paper shredder.

Work did not give Annie the same joy as before. Every morning she showed up automatically two hours before the museum opened its doors to the public. She performed all her usual tasks with compunction and efficiency, but with no pleasure at all. And yet an important change had taken place for her at the museum. These days she would often stop in the hallways to talk to other employees, instead of hurrying past them as before. She was still treated with formality and respect, but a subtle warmth was beginning to show. People smiled at her more often, even if they still addressed her politely as "Miss Brooke."

Now Annie restlessly scraped her chair back and stood up. Her nerves were especially jittery today, and she knew why. Tomorrow morning the board of trustees would convene for a meeting. Both Vance Forester and Annie would give a presentation to the board on their ideas for the future of the museum. And then the board would vote to decide on a new director. It was arriving at last—the moment when she'd have a chance at attaining her dreams. But that wasn't the real reason she felt so jumpy. Tomorrow she would see Derrek again, and that was all she could think about.

She paced back and forth over the Persian rug. What would she say to him? "Hello, Derrek, you've ruined my life. Nothing will ever be the same again." Or, "Hello, Derrek, I can't live without you, so I'm going to give up everything, after all."

Annie leaned her forehead against one of the bookshelves. Derrek had helped her to express her feelings for other people; the coldness deep within her had started to melt under his warmth. Yet he'd asked her to give up her dedication to the museum! Anger surged inside her, and she began pacing again. She had worked so hard to reach this point in her career. If Derrek honestly loved her, then he'd respect that. He wouldn't ask her to toss aside all her dreams for him.

She brought her hand down on her desk, making the pencils rattle in her papier-mâché pencil holder. Her attitude had badly deteriorated these past few weeks, because she hadn't been able to think of anything but Derrek. She'd almost convinced herself that Vance Forester would get the job of director. But she wasn't going down without a fight, that was certain. She'd come this far; she would put everything she had into getting the position herself.

Annie glanced at her watch and then grabbed her purse. She still had time to gather every weapon she could for the trustees' meeting tomorrow.

THE NEXT MORNING Annie peered into the mirror of her medicine cabinet. The glass was so old that it had achieved a permanent fogginess. It would have to do, however; it was the only one in the apartment. Annie set her eye shadow, mascara and lipstick on the bathroom sink. She copied all the deft strokes Charlotte had taught her. Then she swept her hair away from her face, making no effort to disguise her high strong forehead. Her stomach felt queasy with nervousness, and she took several slow breaths to steady herself. In only a few hours' time she would be confronting Derrek and the other trustees.

From a hanger in her closet Annie took down the camel gabardine skirt she'd bought on sale the year before. It was modeled like a riding skirt, with soft folds, an inverted pleat in front and subdued camel buttons all the way down to the hem. It had an understated elegance, but Annie was going to liven it up a bit. From another hanger she took the blouse she'd purchased yesterday and slipped it on. It was a softly tailored silk in a vivid turquoise blue.

Annie wanted to get a good view of herself, so she dragged a chair into the bathroom and stood on it. The foggy mirror of the medicine cabinet allowed her to see only the bottom half of her blouse and the top half of her skirt. But she was convinced that the colors were perfect together. She was part new Annie, part old Annie, and the combination felt just right. She clambered down from the chair and slid into her new camel pumps. Annie walked around the bedroom a few times, getting used to the shoes. All her life she'd owned one pair of good shoes at a time, not buying another pair until they'd worn out. The navy pumps had served her well for more than a year. But then she'd met Derrek, and suddenly her life was overflowing with new shoes.

Now she hesitated in front of her bureau, looking at the turquoise heart laid out on top of it. Why should she ever wear this necklace again? But she couldn't stop her fingers from picking up the slender silver chain. The turquoise stone had lovely variations of blue green; Annie's blouse looked as though it could have been spun from one of those threads of color in the stone. She reached up and clasped the chain behind her neck, trying to convince herself she was only wearing the necklace because it complemented her blouse.

She went to the kitchen and took three sips of water. With that as her only sustenance, she gathered up the poster-board charts she'd made the night before. It was time for her to go to the museum.

ANNIE ENTERED the conference room. It had once been Caroline Darcy's dining room, and still seemed better suited for a dinner party than a business meeting. The long polished table looked as if it needed place settings in china and crystal, and perhaps a floral centerpiece. Instead there were folders scattered over it, along with notepads and pens. The trustees were milling around the table and their faces blurred as Annie stood in the doorway, watching them.

But then one face came sharply into focus. Derrek's. He sat with an arm hooked around his chair back, wearing a suit jacket that was expensive and well cut but slightly threadbare. He had worked one finger between his neck and shirt collar, as if his tie was strangling him and he couldn't wait to yank it off. Annie smiled a little.

Derrek didn't smile back. He gazed at her with an expression she couldn't fathom—serious, almost brooding. Was it just his tie that was bothering him, or the sight of her? She fingered the turquoise heart, wondering if her neckline was too low. Maybe her lipstick was smeared, and that was why Derrek's eyes lingered on her mouth.

Annie became aware that she'd been standing here staring at Derrek for far too long. She wrenched her eyes away from him and walked to the head of the table. The only sound in the room came from two trustees who were riffling through their notepads. The place was oppressive and stuffy, with heavy maroon draperies hanging at the windows. Annie wished she could have seen Vance's presentation to know what she was up against. Her hands were shaking as she placed her poster-board charts facedown on the table. Her mouth felt as if it had been lined with cotton, and even though she wasn't looking at Derrek she could feel the pressure of his gaze.

She cleared her throat. "Gentlemen," she began as the other trustees took their seats, "the Caroline Darcy Museum is ready for change, but that change must also reflect the past we labor to preserve." She'd rehearsed her lines several times in front of the bathroom mirror, making sure they rang with conviction. But now her voice sounded stiff and flat to her ears. She propped up her first piece of poster board and cleared her throat again. "I'd like to introduce all of you to the Darcy Museum Complex—an idea for the future, as well as for the past."

On the poster board Annie had used magic markers to draw several geometric figures: a red square represented the Darcy mansion, a larger green square was the new park she envisioned, and an orange rectangle represented the mill building. She'd got carried away, filling in the green square with little stick trees and bushes; triangles of different colors and sizes indicated where the playground equipment would be. She'd divided the orange rectangle with blue lines, showing where classrooms and exhibits would be placed in the mill building. A small yellow square was parked outside the mill, with purple letters that identified it as the Museum Mobile.

Looking down at her poster now, Annie felt mortified. She'd been so determined not to repeat the mistakes of her ponderous thirty-page report that she'd gone too far in the other direction. This looked like a kid's drawing. Somehow Annie made herself go on talking, pointing to her ridiculous squares and triangles, explaining what they meant. She was floundering, and the faces in front of her blurred more than ever.

Without wanting to, she focused on Derrek again. He was leaning forward in his chair, his elbows propped on the table. He pointed a thumb upward in a discreet but unmistakable sign of encouragement. A warm feeling went through Annie, buoying her up. She remembered what Derrek had told her after the fund-raiser. He'd told her she had empathy, and not to lose that quality just because she was in a crowd.

Annie glanced around the table. She concentrated on one of the faces, and found that she was looking at Sam Dawson. Mr. Dawson was an untidy rumpled man with a mischievous face. Half-forgotten facts about him flowed into Annie's mind now. He had five children and was the kind of father who loved to go trick-or-treating. His own Halloween costumes were always wilder than the ones his kids wore. Disneyland was his favorite vacation spot, and he dragged his protesting teenagers there every year along with his younger kids. He'd once confessed that he liked having so many children because it gave him an excuse to do all the fun things in life.

Annie smiled directly at Mr. Dawson and went on speaking. "The Caroline Darcy Museum Complex would give us an opportunity to encourage creativity in both children and adults. We would have art classes for people of all ages. Imagination isn't something we lose just because we grow older. We can always discover something new and exciting about ourselves and the world around us."

Sam Dawson was definitely looking interested, but Annie didn't want to lose the rest of her audience. She looked across at Harvey Underwood, a mournful, long-faced man who always spoke tragically of the museum's lack of funds. Annie flipped to her chart that showed how cost-efficient the new complex would be. She held it up, gazing at Mr. Underwood and elaborating on how museum revenues would be increased by her plan.

By the time Annie had finished her presentation, she was no longer thinking about the trustees as a formless intimidating mass. All the faces around the table belonged to unique individuals. It was a wonderful revelation and she owed it to Derrek. Annie gathered up her posters, glancing at him. But he didn't look back at her; he was deep in conversation with mournful Mr. Underwood. Annie felt at a loss, wanting to linger so that she could talk to Derrek herself. But the trustees would be taking their vote now, and she had to leave the conference room.

Annie waited impatiently in her office. She didn't even make an attempt to tackle the paperwork on her desk. She hoped fervently that Derrek would come to see her after the meeting. All she could think about was talking to him, feeling his arms around her again. She lined up her paper clips in ordered rows on the desk. They were the plastic kind that came in a rainbow of colors. After Annie had made rows, she rearranged the paper clips into long squiggly lines that looked like variegated snakes.

A knock came at her door. Annie sprang from the desk, paper clips flying.

"Come in," she said, her voice squeaking. But it wasn't Derrek. Mr. Bessler bustled into the room, his silver hair sticking up as if he'd been pulling it.

"Is the meeting over?" Annie asked eagerly.

"Yes, yes. Miss Brooke—"

She started toward the door. "The trustees—they can't be gone yet," she said.

"They left a little while ago."

Annie stopped. "All of them?" she asked.

Mr. Bessler rocked on his feet. "Yes, yes, all of them."

Annie wanted to race out to the parking lot and search for Derrek. He *couldn't* leave like this. She had to stop him!

But if he'd wanted to see her, he would have come to her office. Annie slowly headed back to her chair and sat down again, a cold weight settling in the emptiness of her stomach. Mr. Bessler perched on the edge of a chair across from her. Even sitting down he looked as though he was about to go bouncing off somewhere.

"Miss Brooke, I'd like to congratulate you," he said. "In a majority vote, the trustees have chosen you as the new director of the museum."

Annie lifted her head, knowing that she should feel elated. This was it at last, all her dreams come true. But she experienced no sense of joy, no exuberance— only a dull ache. She felt cheated. For such a long time she had imagined this moment and how she would react. But all that seemed to matter now was the fact that Derrek hadn't come to her.

Mr. Bessler tapped his fingers against his knees. "Several of the trustees told me how much they enjoyed your presentation, Miss Brooke. They asked why you'd been hiding your talents. This truly is a victory for you."

"Thank you, Mr. Bessler." She tried, but she couldn't inject any enthusiasm into her voice. He didn't seem to notice.

"Unfortunately, there has been some, er, unpleasantness. Vance came into my office just now and tendered his resignation. He stated rather categorically that he does not wish to work for you."

Annie felt only relief at this news. "Mr. Bessler, I'm sure everything will fall into place."

He was inching closer and closer to the edge of his chair, until Annie was afraid he might fall off it.

"The trustees are quite enthusiastic about your museum complex, Miss Brooke. In fact, you've been asked to contact a firm at this address today, so you can begin discussing renovations of the mill." He pushed a slip of paper across the desk toward her.

Annie frowned at it. "That was a decision I planned to make myself—who should work on the restoration."

Mr. Bessler gave her a rueful smile. "Miss Brooke, you'll find that juggling politics with the trustees is going to be one of your biggest jobs. Frankly I'm glad it's going to be your headache now, and not mine. I'm going to spend the next few years relaxing on my fishing boat."

Annie glanced at him in surprise. She couldn't imagine Mr. Bessler sitting quietly for hours and hours, with nothing to do but hold a fishing rod. Right now his eyes were darting around as if looking for something new to latch on to. Nothing in Annie's office seemed to catch his interest, however.

He sprang up and hurried to the door. "Again, my congratulations to you, Miss Brooke. I'm sure the future looks very bright to you today."

Annie watched him bustle away, the weight inside her growing heavier. Without Derrek, the future did not look bright at all.

THE ADDRESS Mr. Bessler had given to Annie wasn't far from the museum. She drove to it and parked her car across the street. For a moment she just sat behind the steering wheel, unable to summon the enthusiasm to climb out and talk to anyone about the mill. Such a short time ago, restoring the mill had been the only thing she could think about. Derrek had changed all that.

With a sigh Annie got out of the car and crossed the street. She was in a business district that she'd always liked, where old brick stores had been refurbished and preserved. Now they housed boutiques, antique shops, professional offices for lawyers and accountants. Annie stopped in front of the address on her slip of paper. A workman was stenciling a sign onto the glass door. She stared at the old-fashioned Gothic lettering: D. F. Richards, Arch. The sign ended there, but the workman was laboriously beginning to fill in an *i*. He paused and tipped his spattered hat to Annie, motioning toward the sign.

"Looks pretty good, doesn't it?" he asked. "I do quality work, even if I do say so myself. Wait—don't go away. I wanted to give you my business card. Schuster and Sons, Sign Painters . . ."

Annie fled halfway down the block, questions flying wildly through her head. Derrek, moving to Denver—was that possible? Had he done that for her? She leaned against the window of an antique store, her breath coming almost in a sob. The realization hit her now with terrifying force. That night in her apartment she'd given Derrek so many arguments—he was rushing her into a decision, he was asking too much of her. But deep down was her biggest fear, the real reason she had denied him. She was afraid that she couldn't make him happy, that he would be disappointed in her.

Annie pressed her hand against the shop window and looked at the collection of old music boxes behind the glass. She had a choice now. She could keep running away from Derrek, or she could face her fear.

After a long moment, Annie straightened. She walked slowly back down the street until she was in front of the sign painter again. He seemed pleased to see her.

"Here's my business card," he said. "Schuster and Sons—I'm Schuster. Three sons in the business with me. Not bad, if I do say so myself."

Annie went through a foyer where the carpet had been torn up. She emerged into a large sunny office that had several new file cabinets here and there, and a drafting table pushed up against a window. Derrek's tie and jacket were tossed carelessly over a chair.

He turned from one of the file cabinets and regarded her seriously.

"Annie—"

"No, Derrek. Let me do the talking." She clutched her purse as if it held all the answers. But she had to do this on her own, without any props. Annie set her purse down on the chair, next to Derrek's tie. She stood there before him, as tall and straight as she could make herself. Her heart was pounding in terror; never had she done anything so difficult. "Derrek, I love you," she said, her voice catching. "It's as simple as that. My work, being director of the museum, none of that means anything without you. I have to be with you, no matter what happens. It doesn't have to be here. We'll go to New Mexico—anywhere, as long as we're together. But if you change your mind about me, I'll understand. You can have a grace period—you know, a time to decide if I'm really what you want—" She mumbled the last words against Derrek's chest, for he had gathered her close in his arms. He was chuckling in that deep vibrant way of his.

"Oh, Annie, my love. You make yourself sound like a washing machine with a ninety-day warranty. I love you so much. Can't you see that?"

"It helps to hear you say you love me." Her voice was muffled against his chest. "But I'm so afraid I'll disappoint you! I've never really been with a man before..." The words came out awkwardly, and she tried again. "I've never had a physical relationship with a man, or an emotional one. What if there's something wrong with me?" She couldn't go on, and pressed herself even closer to Derrek.

"Annie, there's nothing at all the matter with you," he said. "You're a warm caring person, and you have to start believing that about yourself. You've given me so much of your warmth already." He raised her face to his and kissed her thoroughly. Then he grinned down at her. "Now that I have my arms around you again, I'm never letting you go. And I'll gladly tell you a hundred times a day that I love you, so you'll never forget that I do."

She smiled back at him, then said, "Derrek, you really didn't have to move your office up here to Denver. We'll work something out."

He smoothed a tendril of hair away from her cheek.

"Seems to me it's already worked out," he said cheerfully. "I'm going to marry the magnificent new director of the Caroline Darcy Museum. You were so good in that meeting! Vance Forester didn't stand a chance. Annie, I never meant to ask you to give up your passion for your work. I was trying to push you again, make you see that we belonged together."

"Derrek, I *have* used the museum as a hiding place. But now that I'm here with you, I don't feel like hiding anymore." Her fingers moved over the soft cotton of his shirt. She couldn't get enough of him—she needed to feel him and to taste him. She reached her hands up and tightened them behind his neck. "Kiss me again," she murmured.

It was a long while before she allowed him to speak. When his mouth lifted from hers, they were both breathless and trembling.

"Annie, you've changed my life," he said huskily. "You were right about everything—how I'd been protecting my mother too much. I didn't want to admit it at first. I guess I wanted to believe that I could still make some sense out of my father's tragedy. But she's the one who has to do that, just as you said. I called her up in Boston and had a good long talk with her. I told her I was moving to Denver right away, and the foundation needed her. She's already back in Santa Fe, and she's digging into the work. You'll meet her soon—she's also going to take over my job as trustee of the museum. I need to be as free as possible to work on the restoration of the mill with you—if you'll let me."

That was almost too wonderful to imagine, working side by side with Derrek, sharing her dreams with him.

She gazed up at him. "Derrek, please tell me if this is what you really want to do," she said earnestly. "What about your work in New Mexico?"

"I can fly down there whenever I need to. And I can design buildings anywhere, Annie. Just give me a good drafting table and I'm set. All I really want is to be with you." His arms tightened around her. "I want to wake up next to you every morning for the rest of my life. I want to look over and see your face on the pillow next to mine. I don't know how long I can wait for that."

"Let's not wait, then," she declared, feeling reckless and lighthearted. She knew exactly what she wanted to do now. It was something spontaneous, passionate and very, very right. She smiled at Derrek. "We're going to take Betsy and fly to Las Vegas," she announced. "Today—right this minute! We're going to get married. And afterward we're going to call Mr. Bessler and tell him we're on our honeymoon. What do you say to that?"

He laughed joyously. "I say yes, Annie Brooke. Betsy and I would be most honored to comply with your request."

"I love you, Derrek." She savoured the words on her tongue, knowing that she'd be saying them a lot from now on. The happiness inside her was deep and sure. She lifted her face to him. "Kiss me again, Derrek," she said softly, and then she smiled. She was going to be saying those words a lot from now on, too.

HARLEQUIN
Romance®

Coming Next Month

#3073 BLUEBIRDS IN THE SPRING Jeanne Allan
After the death of her mother and stepfather, Tracy could have done without a bodyguard—especially Neil Charles. Attractive but arrogant, he clearly held Tracy's wealthy image in contempt. They sparred constantly but she fell in love with him just the same.

#3074 TRUST ME, MY LOVE Sally Heywood
Though it went against her nature, Tamsin had every incentive to deceive Jake Newman on her employer's behalf. Yet when it came to the crunch, she found that Jake's trust in her was the only thing that mattered.

#3075 PLACE FOR THE HEART Catherine Leigh
Florida real-estate developer Felicity Walden knows the Dubois family's Wyoming ranch would make a perfect vacation resort—but Beau Dubois refuses to sell. Still, she's convinced that a cowboy's stubbornness is no match for an Easterner's determination. Even though the cowboy is far too handsome for the Easterner's peace of mind....

#3076 RAINY DAY KISSES Debbie Macomber
Susannah Simmons knows what she wants—career success at any cost. Until she falls in love with Nate Townsend. But her five-year plan doesn't leave room for romance, especially with a man who seems to reject all the values Susannah prizes so highly.

#3077 PASSPORT TO HAPPINESS Jessica Steele
Jayme should have been devastated when she found her fiancé in another woman's arms. But there was no time to brood over the past. She was too busy coping with presently being stranded in Italy in the hands of attractive Nerone Mondadori....

#3078 JESTER'S GIRL Kate Walker
The moment he set foot in her restaurant, Daniel Tyson antagonized Jessica Terry. Though she reacted to him as a stranger, there were two things she didn't know. One was Daniel's unusual occupation; the other was that they'd met—and fought—once before.

Available in September wherever paperback books are sold, or through Harlequin Reader Service:

In the U.S.
901 Fuhrmann Blvd.
P.O. Box 1397
Buffalo, N.Y. 14240-1397

In Canada
P.O. Box 603
Fort Erie, Ontario
L2A 5X3

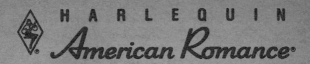

HARLEQUIN
American Romance®

THE LOVES OF A CENTURY...

Join American Romance in a nostalgic look back at the Twentieth Century—at the lives and loves of American men and women from the turn-of-the-century to the dawn of the year 2000.

Journey through the decades from the dance halls of the 1900s to the discos of the seventies ... from Glenn Miller to the Beatles ... from Valentino to Newman ... from corset to miniskirt ... from beau to Significant Other.

Relive the moments ... recapture the memories.

Look now for the CENTURY OF AMERICAN ROMANCE series in Harlequin American Romance. In one of the four American Romance titles appearing each month, for the next twelve months, we'll take you back to a decade of the Twentieth Century, where you'll relive the years and rekindle the romance of days gone by.

Don't miss a day of the CENTURY OF AMERICAN ROMANCE.

A CENTURY OF
AMERICAN ROMANCE
1900's

The women...the men...the passions...
the memories....

CAR-1

A BIG SISTER
can take her places

She likes that. Her Mom does too.

HARLEQUIN SUPPORTS BIG SISTERS
For more information, contact your local Big Brothers/Big Sisters agency.

BIG BROTHERS
BIG SISTERS
OF AMERICA

BIG BROTHERS/BIG SISTERS AND HARLEQUIN

Harlequin is proud to announce its official sponsorship of Big Brothers/Big Sisters of America. Look for this poster in your local Big Brothers/Big Sisters agency or call them to get one in your favorite bookstore. Love is all about sharing.

BB/BS-1A

Harlequin Superromance®

THE LIVING WEST

Where men and women must be strong in both body and spirit; where the lessons of the past must be fully absorbed before the present can be understood; where the dramas of everyday lives are played out against a panoramic setting of sun, red earth, mountain and endless sky....

Harlequin Superromance is proud to present this powerful new trilogy by Suzanne Ellison, a veteran Superromance writer who has long possessed a passion for the West. Meet Joe Henderson, whose past haunts him—and his romance with Mandy Larkin; Tess Hamilton, who isn't sure she can make a life with modern-day pioneer Brady Trent, though she loves him desperately; and Clay Gann, who thinks the cultured Roberta Wheeler isn't quite woman enough to make it in the rugged West....

Please join us for HEART OF THE WEST (September 1990), SOUL OF THE WEST (October 1990) and SPIRIT OF THE WEST (November 1990) and see the West come alive!

SR-LW-420-1